Loving AGAINST THE Pattern

LaKisha Ridley

This is a work of fiction inspired by real-life experiences. Names, characters, locations, and identifying details have been changed to protect privacy. Any resemblance to actual persons, living or deceased, is purely coincidental.

This story reflects themes of struggle, faith, and redemption and is not intended to depict any individual's life in exact detail.

Published by LaKisha Ridley Publishing

Dedication

To God,

For never leaving me, even when I didn't know what I was doing.

To my children and my husband,

Thank you for your love, your listening ears, and for being my reason to keep going.

To my Daddy,

Thank you for instilling in me that I can do anything I set my mind to.

To my Mommy,

We may not have had the relationship we both deserved...but we loved each other the best way we knew how. This book is for you.

I love you. Rest easy.

And to anyone learning to love against the pattern—

keep going.

Acknowledgments

To my Bishop,

Thank you for your spiritual guidance and for always encouraging me to become more.

To Mother Limousine,

In loving memory,

The last words you said to me were, “Baby, tell your story.” Well… here it is.

Table of Contents

Chapter 1: The Night Everything Shifted 1

Chapter 2: Just Kicking It.. 9

Chapter 3: What Feels Good Feels So Bad 19

Chapter 4: Love Taught Me Fear..................................... 29

Chapter 5: Things Done In The Dark 41

Chapter 6: Bad News Perfect Timing 57

Chapter 7: God Brought It Back.................................... 77

Chapter 8: Walking Into Something 85

Chapter 9: It Was Getting Real 99

Chapter 10: Enough Is Enough 109

Chapter 11: The Truth Was In The Bag 117

Chapter 12: Two Lines 125

Epilogue.. 133

Author's Note 137

Author's Bio 139

PRAISE FOR
LOVING AGAINST THE PATTERN

"Loving Against the Pattern really had me thinking. I liked how it showed how past experiences can affect the way you love and the choices you make. It felt real, a little emotional, and I loved the spiritual touch throughout.

Definitely one of those reads that sticks with you—I'm already ready for part two."

- Glenda Jackson

Introduction

I didn't write this book to expose anyone. I wrote it because silence almost broke me. Ever since I was old enough to write and spell my name, I learned early how to survive, how to smile through pain, how to pray without question and how to keep family secrets, and call it loyalty. What I didn't know then was that survival is not the same as healing. This book is my journey out of that silence to through one voice shaped by memory reflection, and survival.

CHAPTER 1

THE NIGHT EVERYTHING SHIFTED

Monique was seventeen and certain that life had just begun. Graduation day was fun. It ended with applause, photos and proud smiles. Monique was happy, really happy. She had graduated from high school a year early and now she had just graduated from flight attendant school. Her family filled the seats, clapping loudly, calling her name. For once, she felt seen. Accomplished. Proud of herself in a way she didn't always allow.

She didn't get certified as a flight attendant like she thought she would due to being under the age of 21. She told herself this was just the beginning. However, she did walk away with a certificate in Transportation Management. At the time, that still felt like a win.

After the graduation was over and her parents headed back home, which was like an hour and a half away from where the graduation ceremony was held. Her parents assumed she would go back home with one of them but Monique had other plans. It was finally time to celebrate. Time to hit the streets.

"Monique and her friend Shanice changed clothes and headed down Crenshaw." The "Shaw" is what we call it".

As Shanice drove down the crowded streets, I couldn't believe what I was seeing. Low riders rode by blasting music and hopping up and down like they were part of the show. Girls in Daisy Dukes and skimpy tops danced in the streets, eating, drinking from red plastic cups, just having a good time. Shanice and I were laughing soaking in all the people that were out that weekend. Shanice was a bold one. She will pull right next to a car and start talking to the boys like she already knew them. I sat back and laughed at all the trash talking and boasting that Shanice was doing. That was just her.

When we passed the Wienerschnitzel, Shanice spotted a gang of boys standing by a Land Cruiser. Before I knew it, she busted a U-turn and parked right behind them. I was shocked at how quickly she hopped out of the car and walked straight over to where they were. A few minutes later, someone handed her a drink, in a red plastic cup. I stayed in the car. I was too shy to be surrounded by all those boys.

Well, Shanice was talking and drinking, I was peeping the scene. I noticed one of the guys from the Land Cruiser walking in the direction of the car. I thought he was headed to the car behind us so I didn't really pay him any attention. When he tapped on the window and told me to roll it down, I was shocked for a second. I thought Shanice had sent him over to grab a pen or something.

When I rolled the window down, there was this fine, ass boy standing there asking me what my name was? "Monique," I said, trying not to sound nervous. He shook my hand and said, "Marcus."

"Hi Marcus, you have really pretty eyes." He smiled and said they were contacts. I laughed and said, "Yeah right." I wasn't the flirty type, but with him, I couldn't help myself.

"How old are you?" I asked. "Nineteen," he said.

He asked me as well, but I didn't get the chance to answer him because we were distracted by sirens with red and blue lights flashing in our direction. Everything changed at once, people started running back to their cars, tossing red cups to the ground, engines were roaring as they sped off. Somehow, in the midst of all the chaos, we still managed to exchange numbers before he disappeared.

It was too late for me to catch the bus home after cruising the Shaw, so Shanice's mom insisted that I spend the night with them. As we rode to her house, we laughed and teased each other about the people we met that night. I couldn't stop thinking about Marcus. Even with all the chaos and sirens, those brown eyes stuck in my head. What was it about him? He didn't look like the other boys—he was a little thuggish, but calm and that smile… oh yeah, that smile got me.

Shanice was laughing beside me, teasing like she always did. "Girl, you're blushing! I saw it!"

I rolled my eyes. "I am not."

She just smirked, shaking her head. "Uh-huh. Sure you're not."

I tried to focus on the street again, but every time I saw a Land Cruiser, I thought of him. Why did I let him get to me like that? I wasn't usually the type to flirt with boys, but with him, I didn't even try to stop myself. We even gave a few of them nicknames like Land Cruiser and Brown Eyes. Those were the two boys we clicked with the most.

To be honest, I didn't hear from Marcus for the rest of the night. In fact, he didn't call me until the next day, Monday evening after he got home from work. I almost didn't answer the call because I didn't recognize his grandmother‘s name when it appeared on my caller ID, but the second I heard his voice, I couldn't stop blushing.

"May I speak to Monique?" he asked.

"This is her." I said.

"This is Marcus. I met you on the Shaw."

"Hey," I said. "How was your day?"

He replied, "It was long! I had the hardest time getting up this morning for work. I was so tired." "Now that I'm talking to you I'm no longer sleepy".

" Yeah I don't see how you made it to work." "Lucky for me. I had the day off." " I stayed up pretty late last night thinking about everything that happened." "Graduation, cruising on the Shaw was so fun!" "Meeting you with those pretty brown eyes was the highlight of my night." I can tell Marcus was blushing from the chuckle he made.

We found out that we have a lot in common. We both like fruity pebbles cereal, we are both the oldest kids and we are both Capricorns. Throughout the conversation, we also discovered that we both like oldies. This caused us to play different songs for one another to see if the other one heard or liked it. We laughed and talked for hours. I don't recall when we dozed off, but I do remember us waking up to his alarm clock sounding off early the next morning to wake him up for work. Neither of us said much at first, we just started laughing. We couldn't believe we were on the phone all night long.

" I gotta get ready for work," he said. "I'll call you later."

I smiled and said, " OK, have a good day at work."

We finally hung up and I laid there staring at the ceiling, still hearing his voice in my head. Lying there after the call ended, I knew I needed to be honest with myself. As much as I liked Marcus, my life wasn't simple. I already had a boyfriend—well, a fiancé—who was incarcerated in Colorado. We had talked about getting married when he got released.

I was upfront with Marcus about it. I didn't want to start anything based on lies. Still, no matter how hard I tried, I couldn't stay away from him. Feelings for Marcus grew fast! Eventually I told my fiancé about Marcus too! He wasn't happy, but he said he understood. He knew I was young and that it wasn't fair for me to wait years for someone who wasn't there.

"But even with all the confusion in my love life, I had already spent most of my life learning how to stand on my own." I had been living on my own for some time. I have lived in a small bachelor apartment since I was sixteen. Before graduating from flight attendant school, I worked and went to school in Hollywood—nearly a two-hour bus ride each way. It wasn't easy, but I was used to taking care of myself.

After I graduated high school a year early, my Dad told me I needed to either get a job or go to college somewhere. He wouldn't allow me to stay in his house doing nothing. That was the green light I needed to leave California City.My mom had arranged for me to stay with her best friend and her husband, to be closer to the flight attendant school but that situation didn't last long. Her husband used to touch me in ways that made me uncomfortable. When I finally told my mom, she took his side. I couldn't stay there anymore. My dad stepped in and co-signed for my first apartment in Lakeview Terrace. That little apartment became my safe space.

That's where I was when Marcus called. Independent. Guarded. Carrying more than most people knew and somehow, still hopeful.

CHAPTER 2

JUST KICKING IT

By the time Marcus and Monique finally saw each other again weeks had passed since the night on the Shaw. Weeks of phone calls that never felt long enough. They talked every day. Sometimes about nothing at all. Sometimes about everything. Marcus wasn't thrilled about Monique being engaged but he kept calling and she kept answering.

They agreed to meet at Monique's apartment in Lakeview Terrace. It was a small bachelorette apartment, but it was hers. She was learning early how to survive, how to keep moving, how not to rely on anyone and how to manage money. Even so, the thought of being alone with Marcus made her nervous, not afraid, just cautious. Although they have been talking for weeks, Monique wasn't completely comfortable being alone in the apartment with him so she invited Lisa. Marcus must have felt the same way because he brought his cousin Quincy.

Lisa showed up first. She always did. She was a slightly older, white, heavy set woman. Her voice was soft, and baby-like, but the way she watched over Monique told a different story. Lisa was protective without being over-bearing, asking questions the way big sisters do curious but never crossing into interrogation. Marcus and Quincy took to her right away.

Quincy looked nerdy at first glance, mainly because of the thick glasses he wore, and the way he dressed conser-vative, almost too put together for their age. Still, he was friendly, flirtatious and laughed often. Marcus on the oth-er hand was quiet and very observant. He didn't drink nor smoke yet somehow he ended up taking a few shots. This was surprising to Lisa because Monique never smoked or drank either but she did. That alone made the night feel easy, comfortable.

They cracked jokes, played music and dominos. Someone suggested a run to the store for some woom wooms and wam wams (snacks). Everyone laughed and peeled out, still buzzing from the easy energy between them all. Monique headed straight for the freezer, yearn-ing for some Chocolate Chip Cookie Dough ice cream.

She stood there, counting the pennies, quarters and dimes in her hand, trying to make sure she had enough money.

Marcus watched her for a moment, then smiled. " You don't have to count your change," he said. " I'll give you the world, if you play your cards right."

Quincy gave him some dap immediately, laughing and giving him props for quoting lyrics from one of the oldies they all played earlier. Monique shook her head, smiling to herself feeling something warm settled in her chest.

Back at the apartment, they watched movies, played games and eventually landed on playing Truth or Dare. Lisa was good at it. She had a way of asking questions that pulled real answers without making anyone feel uncomfortable. When the questions came up about whether Marcus and Monique had kissed yet, they both shook their heads no.

That made it a dare.

They smiled at each other shy, ,blushing, nervous and all at once. Marcus leaned in slowly, giving Monique time to pull away if she wanted.... She didn't. The kiss surprised her. It was soft, slow, more passionate than she expected. It was enough to leave her wondering if it really counted, since it was a dare.

Later, when he leaned in again, it felt different, more intentional. That kiss was deeper, warmer and better than the first one. Monique had to stop it. Not because she didn't want him, because she did. However something inside of her was saying it was the right thing to do. Marcus didn't argue, he didn't question her reasons. He just nodded and pulled back respecting her space she asked for without needing an explanation. That alone made him respect her even more.

Everyone stayed the night. They camped all over the apartment, the floor, sofa and bed. They were laughing like kids who hung out and stayed up all night. The night ended easily. No pressure. No promises. Just long looks and short touches that lingered longer than they should have. The next morning they sat around eating bowls of cereal, joking about the night before as if they hadn't changed anything, even though it changed everything. They all sat around talking, laughing, joking like they'd known each other longer than they actually had. It wasn't forced. Nobody was trying too hard. It just... flowed. They played a few games of Uno and matched a movie or two.

As the night started winding down, everything slowed down too! The laughter faded into softer conversations, then the energy shifted into silence.

I wasn't ready, but I could tell it was time for the moment to end.

"I gotta hit the road and get ready for work tomorrow," Marcus said.

It seemed like Marcus wasn't ready to go either, but he knew he had to. He hugged her once more, longer than necessary, like he was trying to memorize the feel of her arms around him, her small waist, her contagious smile. They walked downstairs, holding hands toward the front gate of the apartment building, neither one wanting the moment to end. Before Marcus released her hand, he planted his smooth, full lips on hers.

It was a nice, intimate kiss... and Monique didn't resist.

"Call me when you get home," she said.

"I will," he promised.

He hugged her one last time before heading to his car.

Lisa and Quincy were off to the side in their own private conversation. They even exchanged numbers.

"My boy really likes Mo", he said.

"I think Monique likes him too!" Lisa said.

"I can tell by the way he looks at her when she's not paying attention." I've never seen him look at anyone like that before." Quincy said.

"Really. I never saw Mo blush this much." Lisa said.

"Well I guess I'll see you again one day." Quincy said.

He gave Lisa a friendly hug and went to the car.

Marcus adjusted into the driver's seat, he turned the volume up, blasting the perfect song as he pulled away. Monique stood at the gate, bobbing her head to the words by Rome:

Every time I see your face makes me want to sing...

Every time I think about your love, it drives me crazy.

That's our song, she thought, watching him until he disappeared from view.

Monique hated to see Marcus leave. Lisa stayed behind to help clean up, picking up cups and straightening things around the room.

"You like him," Lisa said, glancing over at Monique with a small smile.

Monique tried to play it off, grabbing a few things from the table.

"I mean... he's cool," she shrugged.

Lisa let out a soft laugh. "Yeah... okay."

Monique didn't respond. She just kept moving, pretending to focus on cleaning, but her mind was still outside... still replaying the night.

After a while, Lisa grabbed her things and headed out, leaving Monique alone replaying the night over and over in her head. She thought about the way Marcus looked at her, the way he listened, the way he stayed close to her, but never tried to take more than she was willing to give. He was a complete gentleman. Monique was not used to that. He gained major brownie points with her tonight.

———

He called later that evening. They talked like they always did, picking up right where they left off. About the drive. About nothing. About everything. When they finally hung up, Monique laid in bed staring at the ceiling, she caught herself smiling for no reason. Monique swore it was love at first sight — even if she didn't quite understand what loving him would cost her. One thing for sure, that she didn't want to admit.

Seeing him once... hadn't been enough. That's the part that scared me.

———

We kept talking on the phone like nothing had ever changed. Our late night talks turned into longer nights. Our conversations got deeper without either of us trying too hard. It was easy to open up to him. Too easy!

Marcus had a way of making me feel comfortable. I didn't have to pretend to be anything other than who I am. That alone felt different but different didn't always mean safe. I found myself thinking about him more than I wanted to admit. At random times.

At work. On the bus. Laying in bed at night, staring at the ceiling. Little things would remind me of him, and I'd catch myself smiling without even realizing it and then just as fast... something in me would pull back.

Because as good as it felt... something about it didn't sit right. Maybe it was the timing. Maybe it was everything I had just come out of. Or maybe it was the fact that I still wasn't completely free from what I had been dealing with.

Lamond.

Even when he wasn't around...

He was still around.

His presence didn't just disappear because I wanted it to. There were still unanswered questions. Still emotions I hadn't sorted through. Still things that didn't feel finished. That's what made everything with Marcus feel complicated.

Because how do you move forward... when something from your past is still holding on?

I tried not to think about it too much. I tried to just enjoy what was in front of me. I tried to let myself feel something good for once without overthinking it. But my mind wouldn't let me.

Every time I started to get comfortable... that little voice would creep in. Slow down. Don't get too attached. You've been here before. The truth was... I didn't trust myself. I didn't trust my choices. Not after everything I had already been through because what if this was just another situation that felt good in the beginning.... only to turn into something I'd have to recover from later?

What if I was about to repeat the same cycle...

just with a different person? That thought alone was enough to make me pause. Marcus hadn't done anything wrong. Not at all. If anything, he was doing everything right. Maybe that was the problem.

Because I didn't know how to receive that. I was used to confusion. Used to inconsistency. Used to trying to figure things out.

But this? This felt calm. Steady. Genuine.

And instead of relaxing into it...

I questioned it.

Because what feels good... isn't always right.

At least, that's what my past had taught me.

I was unsure if this was something real— or just another lesson waiting to happen.

CHAPTER 3

WHAT FEELS GOOD FEELS SO BAD

Monique laid in bed later that night staring at the ceiling, wide awake even though her body was tired, her mind had lots of energy, it was constantly running. The apartment was quiet, too quiet. Marcus's voice still lingered in her head, the way it always did after they talked. Monique hadn't done anything wrong, not really, but the feelings alone felt like betrayal. Marcus hadn't asked for more than she was ready to give, yet just wanting him felt like crossing a line she had promised herself she wouldn't. She hadn't meant for this to happen. Marcus wasn't supposed to matter this much. The phone calls, the laughter, the way he listened—none of it was part of the plan. Yet here she was, feeling torn in a way she didn't have words for yet.

She smiled without meaning to, then caught herself and frowned. That feeling in her chest—the one that felt warm and exciting—was quickly followed by something heavier.

Guilt.

She rolled onto her side and pulled the covers closer, trying to push the thoughts away, but they came anyway. Thoughts of him slowly turned into thoughts of someone else. Someone she wasn't supposed to forget.

The guilt crept in quietly.

Marcus and Monique became inseparable. They were committed to making time for one another, although they lived quite a distance from each other. They took turns visiting each other. When Monique was off on the weekends, she would catch the bus to LA to spend time with Marcus. When he was off on Sunday Mondays, he would drive her home and stay with That plan worked for their long distance relationship, or whatever it was that they had.

Monique's heart was racing as she stepped off the bus, her bag slung over her shoulder with the headphones to her Walkman around her neck. She scanned the street, looking for Shanice who was blasting her music across the street from the bus stop with her hazard lights on.

Shanice couldn't wait to tease Monique about catching the bus to see Marcus.

"Girl, you're sprung," she said, laughing as they drove off.

Monique's grin stretched wide just from hearing his name.

"I'm not sprung, but he's cool. We're just having fun."

"Yeah right," Shanice said. "How long was that ride? You wouldn't take a long ride like that for just anyone."

"Girl, anyway," Monique said. They both laughed.

"Can you take me to get something to eat before you drop me off? I'll treat you since you picked me up. You saved me from waiting for another bus—that's the least I can do."

"Cool, there's a Burger spot across the street from the Tree Breeze Resort. Do you want to go there before I drop you off to your little boyfriend?" Shanice giggled in the midst of her question.

Monique said yes, trying to hide her excitement of getting closer to see Marcus.

As soon as the girls arrived at the hotel, it was perfect timing. Marcus had just arrived and was getting out of his car.

Before the car stopped, Shanice pulled up on the side of Marcus's car, singing: "Monique and Marcus sitting in a tree... K.I.S.S.I.N.G!"

Both Monique and Marcus started blushing.

"Shut up, girl," Monique said, throwing the paper from her straw at Shanice, laughing. "Thanks for the ride, girl, I'll call you later.

" Shanice drove off.

"Are you tired, Marcus?" asked Monique. "Was the bus ride really long? I would have picked you up if I could have gotten off work earlier."

"I'm fine," she said, though the feeling of butterflies inside gave her away. "It's worth it."

They started walking toward the entrance of the hotel lobby, hands brushing until Marcus finally took hers. It felt natural, right, and wrong all at the same time. She thought of Lamond—how steady, how familiar, how "safe" he had been—but the truth was, safety didn't make her heart race like this.

Marcus held the door open as they stepped into the hotel lobby. The air inside felt cooler, quieter, like the world outside had been put on pause just for them. Monique noticed how he kept checking her out when he assumed she wasn't looking. How he stayed close, not rushing her, not pulling, just there. It made her feel safe and special in a way that surprised her.

They took the elevator up, standing side by side without saying a word. The soft tapping of Monique's short acrylic nails against the elevator wall filled the space between them. When the doors opened, Marcus glanced at her and smiled, that same calm smile that always settled her nerves.

Inside the room, the energy shifted. Not in a loud way—more like a slow awareness. They set their things down, sat on the edge of the bed, and laughed, cracking jokes about minor stuff. The bus ride. Shanice's mouth. How corny the hotel carpet looked. All those long nights of talking on the phone felt completely different now, face to face. It was obvious they were reaching for conversation, trying to bridge the gap between comfort and curiosity.

Marcus reached for her hand, rubbing his thumb against her knuckles.

"I'm glad you came," he said quietly.

Monique swallowed. "Me too!"

She meant it. That was the dangerous part.

He leaned in and kissed her, soft at first, like he was checking in with her before going any further. She kissed him back, her body responding before her mind could catch up. The sweetness of it made her heart beat flutter. She pulled back just enough to breathe.

Her thoughts drifted where she didn't want them to go. Lamond's letters. His handwriting. His promises. The prayers she had whispered the night before, asking God to guide her—to stop her if she was headed down the wrong path.

"God, please don't let me lose myself." She prayed silently.

Marcus didn't push. He searched her face instead, like he could tell something was weighing on her. "You okay?" He asked.

She nodded, even though she wasn't sure that was true. Being there with him felt right—like a feeling she hadn't known she was missing, but just because something felt right didn't make it righteous. She knew that. She felt it in her spirit.

Monique realized then how thin the line was between comfort and consequence and how close she was to crossing it.

"Been thinking about last week," Marcus said, eyes twinkling. "I can't wait for more moments like that." Monique smiled but said nothing, feeling her stomach twist.

"God, help me!" She prayed silently. "Let me do what's right, not just what feels good."

Every laugh, every smile, every shared glance made the world around them fade. Yet Monique felt the weight of Lamond's letters tucked in her apartment, the phone calls she couldn't ignore.

She wanted Marcus, more than she could admit out loud, but she also wanted to do right by God, by herself... and yes, even by Lamond.

It was complicated. Messy. Hard. But she couldn't deny it: being near Marcus was everything she had hoped for—and maybe, a little more than she was ready for.

They didn't rush anything after that. Instead, they laughed it off, like they both needed the break.

"Let's go get some snacks and then come back to the room to play some dominoes," Marcus suggested. Monique felt relieved.

They walked side by side down the street toward the liquor store, the night air cool and calming against her skin. Inside, they wandered the aisles like kids killing time. Marcus grabbed a bag of Lays cheddar chips, Now and Laters, and an orange Crush soda. Monique went straight for the freezer and pulled out a pint of Chocolate Chip Cookie Dough ice cream. She had been craving it all day. She picked it up, then hesitated. At the register, she emptied her bag and began counting loose change—quarters, nickels, a few dimes—hoping it would be enough. Marcus watched her for a moment, amused, then gently pushed her hand aside.

"You don't have to count your change," he said. "You can have anything you want. I got you! I'll give you the world if you play your cards right."

Monique froze, caught between emotions. She felt embarrassed that he saw her counting change again, but also flattered that he still said he'd give her the world, even after she'd stopped him from going any further. An older man standing behind them, dressed sharp in a tan suit with blue Stacy Adams and a matching hat, overheard and laughed.

"That's right, young man," he said. "Let the pretty lady know she could have a good man on her team if she acts right."

Marcus grinned.

Monique shook her head, smiling despite herself, trying not to let the words sink too deep. She knew better than to take them literally—but something about the way he said it melted her heart. Not because she believed him, but because she wanted to.

Back in the room, they got comfortable, snacks scattered between them. The vibe was easy again—jokes, teasing, shared glances that lingered just a second too long. Marcus kept finding reasons to sit closer, not crowding her, just close enough to remind her he was there. He even rested his hand over hers a few times during the domino game.

At one point, Lamond's name flashed across her mind without warning. His letters. His promises. The life she was supposed to be preparing for. The thought of him made her stomach knot.

She caught Marcus watching her, he looked concerned, by softening his expression.

"You okay?" he asked again.

She nodded automatically. "Yeah. Just tired."

It wasn't a lie—but it wasn't the whole truth either. Being there felt right, like a feeling she hadn't known she was missing. But just because something felt right, didn't make it righteous. She knew that she felt it in her spirit. Monique knew at that moment that God had already spoken. What she did next was not done in ignorance. There would be no claiming to be confused later. Couldn't say she didn't know better. This was the warning, the pause. The mercy before the fall. Whatever decision she made from here on out would be hers to carry alone.

As the night went on, laughter filled the room, but something else settled quietly beneath it all. A knowing.

A sense that this wasn't just a moment—it was a turning point. Whether she wanted to admit it yet or not, Monique could feel herself standing at the edge of something she wouldn't be able to undo.

CHAPTER 4

LOVE TAUGHT ME FEAR

Love.

People made it sound so simple. Like it was something soft... something safe. Something you were supposed to want. But that's not what I learned. I didn't grow up watching love. I grew up watching survival. Watching my mama do the best she could with what she had... even when it wasn't much.

Watching her stay in situations that didn't always treat her right. Watching her love people who didn't always love her back the way she deserved. Somehow.... That became normal to me. I told myself I would be different.

That I wouldn't settle. That I wouldn't allow myself to go through the same things she did but life has a way of repeating what you don't heal from.

———

Lamond...

He was a lesson I didn't even realize I was learning. At first, it wasn't bad. It never is. There were good moments. Moments that made me feel like maybe this could be something real.

But over time, things started to shift. Little things at first. Then bigger ones.

The lies.

The cheating, the feeling in my gut that something wasn't right... but not having the proof.

Or maybe I did have the proof... and just didn't want to see it. Because walking away is easier said than done. Especially when you're used to something. Even when it hurts.

That's the part nobody really talks about. How you can know something isn't good for you...

and still stay. Because it's familiar. Because it's what you've seen. Because somewhere deep down, it feels like love—even when it's not.

Lamond didn't just hurt me. He changed the way I saw love. He made me question everything. My judgment.

My choices. My worth, and once that happens.... It's hard to trust again.

Some memories don't announce themselves. They arrive quietly, uninvited, slipping in when the room is too still and the mind has too much space to wander. That night, after seeing Marcus, after the laughter and the warnings she couldn't ignore, Monique laid awake in her apartment staring at the ceiling. The silence felt familiar, too familiar! It reminded her of being a little girl, lying in bed, listening. Back then, silence didn't mean peace. It meant waiting. Waiting to see what kind of night it would be. Waiting to hear her name called in a tone that made her stomach bubble before anything even happened. Monique learned early how to stay still. How to stay ready. How to read moods the way other kids learned to read books. She knew when to speak and when not to. When to move and when to freeze.

She remembered watching her mother's face closely, searching for clues. Trying to predict which version of her she was getting that day. The loving one. The angry one. The one who acted like Monique was the problem just for existing. There were times she wanted to cry but didn't. At times she wanted to run but couldn't show fear. She learned how to swallow feelings whole and keep moving. She learned how to be strong before she even understood what strength really was.

Somewhere along the way, Monique learned another lesson too! One she never realized she was carrying, it was that love wasn't always gentle. Attention didn't always feel safe and being chosen felt less like comfort. It was more like a surprise, something sudden, almost shocking, like it could disappear just as quickly as it came.

Lying there now, years later, she realized something unsettling. Marcus made her feel seen. The way his presence calmed her. The way being close to him made the world feel quieter. It wasn't new. It was familiar and that scared her more than anything else.

When Marcus came into my life.... Things felt exciting. Patient. Consistent. It should've felt right. But it didn't. Not completely. Because I wasn't just looking at him for who he was...

I was looking at him through everything I had already been through and that changed things.

I found myself questioning the good. Waiting for something to go wrong.

Wondering if this was just another situation that looked good in the beginning... only to fall apart later. That's what fear does. It doesn't always show up loud. Sometimes it's quiet.

Sometimes it sounds like: Don't get too comfortable. Don't trust it too much!

Don't fall too fast!

———

Monique lay in bed, staring at the ceiling. Her body was tired, but her mind was wide awake, running through everything it shouldn't. The feeling of butterflies from being near Marcus lingered, yet guilt tugged at her chest. Another part of her hesitation with Marcus had nothing to do with timing or distance, it was trust. Her mind took her to the past with Lamond. He had cheated on her more times than she could count. She stayed anyway. Not because it didn't hurt, but because he was all she knew. Familiar pain felt safer than the risk of learning something new.

Lamond constantly disrespected Mo. Every time, he came back with gifts, apologies, tears—and she forgave him. She fought for him sometimes, too, trying to make him understand she wouldn't stand for being treated that way. There were always other females. Always rumors. Always something she was trying not to see. Each time, he came back the same way, apologies, soaked in tears, arms full of gifts, promises that sounded convincing enough to quiet her doubts. She forgave him more times than she could remember.

Once, it went too far to ignore. She came home and noticed money missing from her top drawer. Later that day, she saw him out with her friend, on a date at Burger King. They acted like it was nothing. To top it off it was Mo's money he stole to take her friend out on a date with. They looked at Mo like she didn't exist. That day Monique saw red, She dragged her friend by her fake pony tail all through Burger King. It was not a pretty site. The betrayal burned so deeply it blurred her judgment from turning the anger on Lamond.

Then there was her mother's voice, one that never fully left her. Her mother's words floated in her head like daggers. She would say things like: "You're ugly with those chickenpox scars on your face." Or "Look at you with those big old dog teeth." Even as a teenager, when her teeth were straightened and the spots on her face faded, when her small waist and athletic thighs gave her a figure people noticed, she still didn't see herself the way the world did. She didn't see the gifts God had given her—the smile that could light a room, the energy that drew people in.

Those words had planted deep, shaping how Monique saw herself. Making her question why anyone would choose her. If your own mother thought you were ugly, why would anyone else think differently? So she questioned anytime someone did show interest, what was it really for? She knew it couldn't be for her looks so, she always wondered how long would that choice last before they saw her the same way her mother did?

Lamond was the first. The first person to maybe, just maybe convince Monique that her mom was wrong about her being ugly or even wanted. He spoiled her with Name-brand clothes, jewelry, shoes and things she never dreamed of having. Things she had never owned before. Each gift felt like proof. Proof that she was worth something, that someone saw her, wanted her. It gave her a small boost of confidence, a feeling she hadn't known how to handle yet.

Lamond's cheating had only made her doubt it more. If someone who was supposed to love her could hurt her, why would anyone else see her worth?

Her father had warned her about him multiple times but she was young, naive, and enchanted by the first person to show her attention, to make her feel wanted. Safety had felt like love, and she didn't yet know the difference.

Now, lying there, her mind flashed back to Marcus. How different he felt. He was respectful, patient and kind. The weight of choice pressed on her.

"God, guide me", she prayed silently. "Don't let me make a mistake." Before she knew it, she was praying out loud:

"Hey God, please guide me down the right path. Don't let me make another decision that will hurt me more than I already have. Help me to choose someone who will truly love me for me. In Jesus's name, I pray Amen,"

The memory of all I'd been through, the love I'd been taught to expect, and the way Marcus made me feel mingled in a tangle of excitement and fear. For the first time, I realized that loving someone didn't have to hurt. But trusting again? That was something else entirely.

After lying on the bed for what felt like hours, Monique finally pushed herself up. She ironed her clothes for work, slid a CD into the stereo, and headed for the shower. As the steam filled the bathroom, she lathered up with her favorite Warm Vanilla Sugar body wash.

Then the music played:

"Alone in a room, it's just me and you..

I feel lost, Lord, 'cause I don't know what to do..."

Yolanda Adams' voice blasted through the speakers, and Monique froze. The timing felt too perfect to be a coincidence. It was as if God, Himself was telling her to talk to Him, to lay everything out and trust that the answers would come. Singing along in the shower, the weight that laid heavy on her chest shifted, stirring thoughts of Lamond... and making her yearn for Marcus even more. She wanted to reach for Marcus, feel his presence, but even thinking about it sent a quick chill through her body. The memory of Lamond, the broken trust, the empty promises, all pressed down on her at once.

Caught between thoughts of the two men, reality settled in. Love didn't always feel gentle. Attention didn't always feel safe. Being chosen had always caught her off guard. Falling in love was easy but getting out of it was hard.

Lamond's letters flashed through her mind, the sweet words, the apologies, the gifts. They had a way of making her feel special, yet trapped, guilty, and confused all at once. She had loved him since she was sixteen years old... or at least what she thought was love. However, what she felt for Marcus was different. He was patient, thoughtful, and respectful. He made her feel wanted, like she could finally breathe without overthinking every moment. He complimented her a lot. You can tell he meant every word of it, just from the way he looked at her.

Her hand pressed against her forehead. She hated how she had been taught to forgive too quickly, to accept betrayal as part of love. With Marcus, every instinct inside her screamed that things could be different, that she could be different. Still, fear whispered in the back of her mind. Could she trust him? Could she trust herself?

She closed her eyes and whispered a prayer.

"God, help me. Show me the right path to follow. Don't let me repeat the same mistakes. Give me the courage to choose what's right, not just what feels good.

Even as she prayed, a part of her ached for the warmth of Marcus's hand, his soft lips against hers, the way his presence made the world shrink down to just the two of them. It was everything she wanted and everything she feared at the same time.

The phone rang loudly on the nightstand. She hesitated before picking it up. Seeing Marcus's number on the caller ID made her heart flutter,not with guilt, but with longing. He doesn't know how torn I am, she thought. He only sees the side of me that wants to be brave. But can I be brave enough to let him in... fully? Monique took a deep breath and pressed her thumb against his number on the screen. The decision to answer was tough.

"Hello..." she said softly.

"Hey, you okay?" Marcus's voice came through, calm and familiar.

For a second, she didn't answer. Because the truth was... she didn't know.

"Yeah," she finally said. "I'm okay."

But even as the words left her mouth, she knew they weren't completely true. They talked for a while about all sorts of stuff, a little bit of this, a little bit of that. Just like they always did. His voice had a way of calming her, making things feel simple again, even when her mind was anything but calm and that scared her.

After they hung up, Monique sat there for a moment, staring at the phone in her hand.

Her heart felt full...but heavy at the same time. She leaned back against the pillows, her mind going in circles. Marcus felt right. Too right! That's what made her pause.

Because everything that ever felt good before... eventually hurt her.

She closed her eyes, letting out a slow breath.

"The truth is..." she whispered to herself, "I don't know if I'm ready."

Ready to trust. Ready to let go of the past.

Ready to believe that something different could actually be real.

This felt too different .... It didn't feel normal to me.

Anything that didn't feel normal made me feel nervous, maybe even a little scared.

CHAPTER 5

THINGS DONE IN THE DARK

The phone rang twice before she answered.

"Hello," Monique said, her voice soft and sleepy, like he'd caught her right in that space between rest and dreaming.

Marcus leaned against the wall, already picturing her. Those dreamy eyes with the natural long lashes, unguarded. The vision of her made him slow down. The one that made him want to be careful. This was the moment. He knew it.

"Hey," he said. "I just wanted to make sure you made it home okay." It's weird but I miss you already."

"I did," she said. "I'm good." I miss you too!

The pause that followed felt heavier than silence. Marcus opened his mouth. Not loud. Not urgent enough to interrupt the call. But urgent enough that his chest tightened.

His other line on his phone beeped continuously. He pulled the phone from his ear and glanced quickly at the caller ID.

Monique had been honest from the start, about her fiancé, about her boundaries, about not wanting to lose herself again. That honesty made him want to be better than the men who had come before him. He hadn't planned on falling for her.

Not like this.

Not without touching her. Not without claiming her.

Definitely not while carrying something that could change everything if he said it out loud.

"I was just thinking about you," he said instead.

She smiled, he could hear it. "Aww that's sweet, "she said

Marcus closed his eyes. There were parts of his life she hadn't seen yet. Things that didn't fit neatly into conversation. Things that came with responsibility, timing, and no rewind button.

He didn't want to hurt her. He didn't want to rush her. Didn't want to become another disappointment wrapped in good intentions. So he stayed quiet.

They talked about nothing important, just work, sleep, the way the night felt too quiet. When the call ended, Marcus stayed where he was, staring at the dark screen in his hand.

It vibrated again. This time, he looked. His jaw tightened. Some truths didn't announce themselves loudly.

They just waited patiently,

unavoidable

until you were brave enough to face what came with them.

Marcus sat on the edge of the bed long after the call ended, so deep in thought that he

didn't realize Quincy was standing near the door, overhearing the entire conversation.

"You couldn't tell her, huh?" Quincy said quietly.

Marcus shook his head and punched the bed with his fist.

"If I tell her, I could lose her before I even get her," he said. "She told me before—this situation would be a turn-off for her." "A deal breaker."

Quincy exhaled slowly. "Man, she might make an exception for you. I don't know what it is, but you two got something special."

After Quincy left, the room went silent. Just crickets. All Marcus could hear were the loud thoughts racing through his head. He stayed seated on the edge of the bed, elbows on his knees, staring down at the floor. Monique had been honest with him from the very beginning—about her fiancé, her boundaries, her fear of losing herself again. That honesty mattered to him more than he had expected. It made him want to move differently with her. Be better.

He wasn't scared of responsibility. He was scared of being another man who hurt her.

He told himself he wasn't lying, just waiting. Waiting for the right time. Waiting until he could explain everything without it sounding messy or careless. Waiting until he knew how to say it without breaking whatever this was between them.

But the truth didn't wait quietly. It pounded in his head, heavy, constant. Tied to a moment before her. Before feelings. Before he ever imagined wanting someone this much.

He could already picture her face if he told her. The way her smile would fade. That look of disappointment in her eyes, not because she was judgmental, but because her perception of him would change. Marcus didn't know if he was ready to see that. He rubbed his hands together slowly and exhaled.

He didn't want to rush her. Didn't want to pressure her.

Didn't want to ruin something that felt real before it even had a chance. But as he sat there, alone with his thoughts, one question kept coming back—

Was he waiting for the right moment...

or just avoiding the courage it would take to face it?

Monique decided to call Marcus back. She had forgotten to tell him earlier that Shanice had invited the both of them to Hawaii with her and Land Cruiser, AKA, Marcus's friend who was with him the night on the Shaw. Shanice found a really good deal for a group of six or more.

Marcus answered on the second ring, forcing his voice to sound normal, even though his chest felt tight. He didn't want her to hear the hesitation. He didn't want her to think something was wrong when everything already felt so fragile.

"Hey," he said casually. "You needed to hear my sexy voice again, huh?"

They both laughed.

"I was calling to see if you heard about the Hawaii trip with Shanice and ya boy," she said. "Do you wanna go? I think it would be fun."

The excitement in her voice made it a little easier for him to act normal.

"Nah," Marcus said. "I don't wanna go. I'm scared to get on planes."

The conversation drifted from there. Her laugh, her goofiness, it made it hard for him to keep the truth buried. Still, he managed to talk like nothing was wrong. They joked about their bosses at work, how tired she was, random little things that didn't matter, but somehow mattered because it was them. Marcus laughed when he was supposed to, responded when it made sense. However inside, his thoughts kept circling the same place. He was carrying something heavy and she had no idea.

He hated keeping a secret from her. Not only did he like her, he considered her a friend, someone he didn't want to lose.

In the middle of her sentence, Monique paused.

"Hold on," she said. "Someone's beeping on my other line."

Marcus's heart skipped. He didn't know why, but the silence stretched longer than he expected.

"I'm sorry," she said, when she came back. "It's... it's him."

Marcus already knew who him was.

"I'll talk to you tomorrow, okay?" she said.

He swallowed. "Yeah. Alright."

And just like that, the line went dead

She hurried to the other line, ending the call.

Marcus stared at his phone, the quietness of the room pressing down on him. He was kinda tripping about how quickly Mo rushed off the phone. Although he knew the situation Mo was in, he still didn't like being second. He thought about calling her back but that thought erased quickly. He wasn't scared of Monique, not really. He was scared of himself. Scared of how this truth could change everything before he had a chance to make it right.

He now felt worse than he had before. Usually, he was the last voice she heard before falling asleep each night. Not Lamond. Not tonight. He didn't expect that—not now, not when he was already drowning in his own thoughts.. Marcus stared at his phone,

Because some truths... don't just wait for the right moment. They wait for you to be brave enough to face them.

Lamond was still there. Still present. Still connected to her life in ways Marcus couldn't compete with yet. Suddenly, the weight of his secret felt even heavier. The truth he was holding back had the power to push her straight back into the arms of the man he was afraid of becoming. He leaned back against the headboard and exhaled. How do you ask someone to trust you... when you're standing in the middle of your own unfinished truth?

Marcus stayed on the edge of the bed long after Monique hung up. His room was quiet now, except for the sound from the fan. Quincy had left, leaving him alone with his thoughts—and the weight of the truth he hadn't shared. He rubbed his hands over his cornrows. Then he stared down at his phone. Part of him wanted to call her again, just to hear her voice one more time. But he knew he couldn't. Not yet. Not until he figured out how to say what needed to be said without messing up everything between them.

Every time he pictured her—that tiny waistline, those thick thighs. The curve of her smile, the way she laughed when she thought no one was watching—he froze. How could he tell her that there was a part of his life she didn't know? That there was something already attached to him that could complicate everything?

He couldn't. Not now! He pressed his palms against his face and exhaled slowly. He told himself he wasn't hiding out of fear. He was protecting her from disappointment, from confusion, from the very kind of pain that had followed her before.

But the truth didn't wait. It never did.

His phone vibrated. He glanced down. Another call. His chest tightened before he even saw the name. He didn't recognize it, and yet the signal felt urgent, too impossible to ignore. Marcus let it ring, pacing the small space between the bed and the window. When he finally answered, it wasn't Monique on the other end—it was someone else, someone that reminded him that the world outside their connection kept moving, kept demanding attention, kept testing the fragility of what he was trying to protect.

Lamond ....

"Man, where is this girl at?" Lamond muttered while the phone rang.

"I've been calling her for the past few days and she ain't answering."

Third ring.

"Hello?" Monique's voice came through, soft but cautious.

An automated voice interrupted.

"You have a collect call from the Colorado Detention Facility.

You have a collect call from—"

"Baby, it's me!" Lamond cut in quickly.

"If you accept these charges, please press one."

A pause. Beep. Connection accepted.

"Hey, Baby," Lamond said,

His voice was smooth and easy — the kind that used to make her heart flutter and now made her stomach twist.

"I've been trying to reach you the past few nights." "Where have you been? I know you saw on the caller ID that I've been calling."

"I've been... busy," she replied carefully, refusing to feed his tone.

"Hmm... yeah, right."

He half-laughed, half-accused.

"You got somebody over there or something?"

"Don't come at me like that," Monique snapped before she could stop herself.

"I'm not the one who cheated multiple times."

Silence. Then a small exhale on his end.

"Alright, bae. You're right! "We ain't gotta bring up the past. I was just mad 'cause I haven't heard your voice lately."

Her jaw tightened. That wasn't an apology. That was repositioning.

"Anyway," he continued, his tone shifting.

"I got some good news. That's really why I've been dying to talk to you."

He paused — dramatic on purpose.

Her heart betrayed her and beat faster anyway.

"Really?" "What?"

"Your man is coming home soon, baby!" he said, excitement bursting through the line. "Can't wait to see my baby... correction — my fiancée."

Monique's fingers tightened around the phone.

Coming home?

She was disappointed, stressed, and obligated.

"When?" she asked evenly.

"In a few weeks," he replied confidently.

Too confident!

"You don't sound excited." He said.

The walls felt like they were closing in on her. She didn't want or need this type of news right now. The echo of her mother's voice immediately slammed into her mind:

"You're ugly." "Nobody will ever want you. With them big old dog teeth in your mouth."

For a moment, she felt so small and pressured. She needed advice, real advice! She couldn't tell her dad — he never liked Lamond and still saw her as a child.

She couldn't tell her mom, that conversation would turn into criticism and she definitely couldn't tell Marcus. Not yet at least.

"Babe, when I get home, I want you to make me some of them good tacos, " Lamond added casually, already picturing himself back in control.

"You have 30 seconds remaining for this call before being disconnected," the operator announced.

Monique swallowed. "Okay."

"That's it?" Lamond asked. "Just okay?"

"I'll talk to you later," she said. Click. The line went dead.

Lamond sat there holding the receiver longer than necessary.

"Something's off. She ain't acting right."

"First she's too busy to answer."

"Now she sounds different, distant!" When has she ever not been excited to see me?

He stared at the wall of the detention facility, jaw tightening.

Meanwhile, Monique stood in her quiet apartment, phone still in her hand.

She exhaled slowly. She felt alone. Alone in decisions. Alone in expectations.

Alone in patterns she never asked to inherit.

Everything inside her screamed that she did not want her mother's life.

But fear whispered,

that this might be her only chance and just like that,

the weight of choices she hadn't fully made settled heavily on her chest.

Lamond ....

Lamond sat still for a moment after the call with Monique ended. Her response just didn't sit right with him. She was too calm, too nonchalant! He reached for the phone again.

Dialed. Ring. Ring, Ring

"Hello"

"This is a call from the Colorado Detention Facility," an operator said.

"You have a collect call from;

"Lamond," he said.

A woman answered, her voice was lower than Monique's, slower, older, more seasoned.

"Your ears must've been ringing." She said smoothly. "I was just thinking about you."

A slow grin spread across Lamond's face.

"Oh yeah? Tiffany wanted to hear Big Daddy's voice, huh?"

Tiffany laughed softly. " You really think highly of yourself."

"I know how I affect women," he continued playfully. "Especially you."

"You must want something," she replied. "You don't just call to say hello."

"Can't a man check on somebody he's been thinking about?"

"Have you?" she asked, not buying it but entertained.

"All day," he lied easily. "You crossed my mind this morning."

"Is that so?" she replied. "Funny, I thought you forgot about me."

"Forget you? Impossible. " His voice dropped slightly. "A woman like you doesn't get forgotten, Tiffany."

Silence. Not awkward. Intentional.

"You always know what to say," she murmured.

"That's 'cause I pay attention to you, baby," he replied. "So... what you got on right now?"

She laughed softly. "You're bold."

"Only when I know I can be."

"What makes you think you can, with me?" She challenged him.

"Because you answered," he said smoothly. "Don't act like you don't both think about some of our nights together."

A pause.

"You're still dangerous," she said quietly.

"Only for the right woman."

"You say that to everybody?" She snapped back.

"Nah. Only the ones that can handle me." He smiled rubbing his hands together.

Another quiet laugh.

"You're something else." She said,

"You like it though." In his cocky voice.

"You keep thinking that." Tiffany laughed.

"I like confidence," she corrected gently. "Arrogance I tolerate."

The operator's voice interrupted: "You have 10 seconds remaining for this call."

"Already?" Lamond muttered. "They are always cutting me off when I'm having a good conversation."

"Maybe that's your sign," she teased.

"Or maybe it's motivation," he countered. "I'll call you again."

"You do that," she said calmly.

Call dropped. Lamond leaned back against the wall, a slow grin forming. Now that's how my woman should sound when I call her.

CHAPTER 6

BAD NEWS PERFECT TIMING

Monique held up a red sundress and waved it in the air.

"Girl, this would look so cute on you."

She stepped closer, pressing the dress against Shanice's frame and squinting like a stylist.

"Oh yeah, that is cute,". Shanice said, turning slightly to check herself in the mirror. "You think this works for Hawaii?"

"Try it on. That's the only way you'll know." Monique smirked. "But definitely put that green and pink bathing suit back. Nothing about it says CUTE.

Shanice gasped dramatically before laughing, tossing a bright pink tank top into the cart.

"Please! I make everything cute," she said with a sly grin.

As she outlined her figure she said, "Hawaii better get ready for Shanice, Baby."

They both laughed — the kind of laugh that made people glance over and smile.

Then Monique snapped her fingers. "Speaking of preparing... I forgot to tell you. Lamond called." "He will be home in a few weeks."

Shanice's smile faded just a little and her eyebrows lifted. "Oh wow. That's soon. Girl, your life is about to be better than any daytime soap opera."

The joke landed — but heavier than Shanice realized.

Lamond coming home was the elephant in every room of Monique's life. The weight she couldn't fold and hang neatly on a rack like everything else. She ran her fingers along the hem of the dress.

"I thought I'd be excited," she admitted quietly. "But I don't know... I just feel pressured."

"Pressured?" Shanice stopped walking and faced her. "Baby, that's not excitement, that's an obligation, a red flag!"

Monique swallowed.

"Are you really about to let him come back and rearrange your whole life again?" Shanice continued, her tone playful but pointed. "You've been glowing lately. Laughing more. Living more."

Monique knew exactly what she meant.

"I hear you," Monique sighed. "But I can't... I don't want to repeat my mom's habits."

Shanice's expression softened — but only slightly.

"You are not your mother. Stop carrying that like it's your inheritance."

Monique looked away.

"But let me ask you something," Shanice added, leaning closer. "Before you shut everything down... are you at least gonna see what you're walking away from?"

Monique blinked.

Shanice grinned.

Cause let me tell you," Shanice continued with a smirk, "if Marcus is anything like Mr. Landcruiser... you would be crazy not to test drive. Monique burst out laughing, swatting her arm. They high-fived like teenagers, drawing a few side-eyes from other shoppers.

"But seriously," Shanice continued, lowering her voice just enough. "Marcus isn't Lamond and whatever this is? It feels and looks different. You at least owe it to yourself to find out."

The laughter faded. Monique's fingers brushed the dress again, but she wasn't really seeing it anymore. Monique froze and her mind drifted away.

Shanice's words lingered.

Marcus.

The way he listened. The way he looked at her like she wasn't something temporary.

Her stomach fluttered — warm, unsettling, alive.

"You're right," she whispered more to herself than Shanice. "Maybe I do need to see what I've been avoiding."

Shanice looped her arm through hers.

"That's all I'm saying. Sometimes you gotta taste the future before the past shows up knocking." Monique let out a quiet breath. Lamond's voice still lived in her memory — confident, familiar, fiancé.

But Marcus? Marcus felt different. Marcus felt like sunlight slipping through blinds after a long storm. Her mind wasn't clear — it hadn't been in months.

But for the first time in a long time...

Her choice didn't feel like fear.

And maybe — just maybe — she was ready to make one.

They found a small table near the window, bags stacked at their feet. Shanice was mid-story about her co-worker when Monique's phone lit up. She glanced at the phone and it read:

Mommy.

Shanice noticed immediately. "Speaking of generational pressure," she mumbled..

Monique smiled automatically as she looked at Shanice.

"Hi Mommy, How are you? Is everything okay?"

"Yes, I'm fine," her mother replied. "What are you doing?"

"Just hanging out with Shanice." Monique replied.

"Oh tell her I said hi."

"Hey Mom's!" Shanice called across the table.

There was a brief chuckle. Then her mother's tone shifted — not cold, but careful.

"I ran into Lamond's mom at the grocery store the other day."

Monique sighed lightly. "Oh yeah?"

"She said, he's coming home soon."

"Yeah, I know."

There was a pause.

""Where's the excitement?" her mother pressed. "Don't start acting unsure now. That man has been committed to you. Do you know how rare that is?"

The word sat heavy.

Her mother continued, "You don't want to throw away something stable chasing temporary feelings."

Shanice was pretending not to listen — but absolutely listening as she cut her eye at me.

"Mommy, it's not about chasing anything," Monique said quietly.

"Well then what is it about?" her mother challenged. "Because from where I'm standing, it looks like fear and fear will have you alone."

That landed. Hard. Monique's fingers tightened around her phone.

"I just don't want to make a decision because I feel obligated."

There was a pause on the other end.

"Obligated?" her mother repeated. "Monique, relationships aren't about butterflies. They're about security. Stability. Building something that lasts."

Monique swallowed.

Security.

Stability

"Anyways, that's not the only reason why I'm calling you. "Mo there's something I've been meaning to tell you. I've hesitated for years. But if he's coming home... and if you're planning a wedding... you need to know."

Monique straightened in her seat.

"Know what?" Monique asked.

"When you apply for a marriage license, they'll ask for your birth certificate."

"Okay... I'll get it from you when the time comes."

"That's not why I'm telling you. "Her mom said in an agitated tone."

Monique's stomach tightened.

"What are you saying Mommy?"

There was silence on the other end.

Then —

"The name listed under father might confuse you."

Monique laughed nervously. "Confuse me how? It says Daddy's name."

Another pause.

"No," her mother said quietly. "It says Phil."

Monique blinked.

"Phil who?"

"Your father's best friend."

Silence.

Monique shook her head automatically. "Okay… so that's a mistake. We'll just get it corrected. That's easy."

"MONIQUE," her mother snapped. "Stop acting naïve and listen to me."

Shanice froze mid-bite.

"I don't understand why you're yelling?" Monique said, her voice tightening.

Her mother inhaled sharply.

"Phil's name is on your birth certificate because… he might be your biological father."

The restaurant noise suddenly felt distant. Shanice's mouth slowly fell open. Monique didn't speak.

Didn't blink.

Didn't breathe.

"What did you just say?"

"Stop acting all stupid and dramatic!" Her mom said in a hostile voice.

Monique rolled her eyes and took a long sigh.

Mommy, I gotta go. Shanice needs my help with the bags of clothes.

"Well don't let Shanice fill your head with foolishness," her mother replied sharply. "Friends don't have to live with your consequences."

"Ok, Mommy, I'll talk to you later. Gotta go"

The call ended with a polite goodbye — but the air felt different.

Heavier.

With the help of Monique, Shanice had finally finished packing for Hawaii. Suitcases lined the driveway like soldiers waiting for inspection. The afternoon sun hit just right, warm but not unbearable. As we waited in front of the house for Marcus and Mr. Landcruiser to arrive so that Marcus and I could drop them off at the airport.

"Girl, you're looking all serious in a deep daze," Shanice teased, snapping her fingers. "I know you're going to miss me and all, but I'll be back soon. Don't get all sad and emotional on me."

"Ain't nobody thinking about you," I shot back, laughing.

"Uh oh, Mo! There goes your song!" Shanice yelled as "You're Making Me High" started bumping through the speaker.

I shook my head no, but Shanice was persistent. She kept tugging at my hands until I had no choice but to join her foolishness. Dancing was not my forte, but she didn't care who was watching — and apparently didn't care if I cared either. She quickly yanked me up from the chair. Next thing I knew, I was lost in the song, dancing.

I rolled my eyes, but Shanice didn't care. She knew I looked foolish, cars honked as they passed, but Shanice didn't stop. I turned my back to the street, laughing despite myself, finally letting the music take over. For a brief second, I forgot about my mother, about the questions. About everything. Marcus stood about a foot behind me, grinning like he'd just caught something priceless on camera. Mr. Landcruiser leaned against the passenger door, chuckling at the scene. Shanice was bent over, laughing so hard she could barely breathe.

Then—

I felt a playful tap on my butt.

"Cut all that out!"

I froze.

Heat rushed to my cheeks. As dark as my complexion is, I think I was turning red. The light tap on my butt was flirtatious, playful — just a bold move for Marcus. Something that made us all laugh, loosening the tension I'd been holding onto all day. Even as I danced, my mind drifted. I knew something had changed. Marcus wasn't just a friend anymore and for the first time in a long while, I wasn't entirely afraid of it.

"Y'all are childish," I muttered, trying to recover what little dignity I had left.

But the laughter spilled across the driveway, easy and familiar.

———

Once the guys loaded the suitcases into the trunk, Shanice pulled me aside.

"Look," she said, lowering her voice. "I know your mom dropped a bomb on you but, don't let what she said mess up your weekend with Marcus."

I looked away.

"Who knows," she added with a dramatic eye roll, "this might be your last chance together before Lamond gets home."

I nudged her shoulder, but the words stuck.

Last chance.

———

On the way to LAX, we all talked over each other, bobbing our heads to the music. Mr. Landcruiser argued about flight snacks. Shanice insisted she was getting upgraded to first class by "manifestation alone."

Marcus laughed, but every now and then his eyes shifted to me.

He knew something was off.

He didn't ask.

Not in front of everyone.

———

After we dropped them off, we stood there for a second watching them disappear into the sliding airport doors.

"Bye y'all! Take pictures!" I shouted.

Then it was just us.

As we pulled away from the curb, the car grew quieter.

"Wanna stop and get something to eat?" Marcus asked.

"I'm not really hungry. But we can if you want."

He glanced at me, then turned the music down without saying anything. That small gesture began to make me nervous.

"I noticed earlier you were acting a little different," he said gently. "Are you okay?"

"I'm good," I replied too quickly. "It's just been a long day."

He didn't argue. Just nodded. But his hand reached across the console and squeezed mine and he left it there.

———

By the time we pulled into the hotel parking lot, my stomach was in knots. The lobby smelled like clean linen and something citrusy. Everything felt calm.

Too calm.

Inside the room, Marcus tossed his keys on the dresser and turned toward me.

"Okay," he said softly. "Now tell me what's really going on."

There was no accusation in his voice. Just concern. I sat on the edge of the bed, staring at my hands.

For a second, I thought about saying nothing.

But then I remembered—

He has always been a friend first. A good listener. Someone who never made me feel dramatic.

"My mom told me something that shocked me earlier today ," I said quietly.

He didn't interrupt.

"She said... there's a possibility that the man I've called Daddy my whole life might not be my biological father."

The words felt heavier saying it out loud. Marcus blinked.

"What?" He said, looking lost for words.

I nodded, my eyes started burning.

"My mom said she planned on taking her secret to her grave. However, since I plan to get married soon, she had no choice but to tell me."

Silence filled the room. Surprisingly, it wasn't awkward, just silence. He walked over slowly and sat beside me.

"Has your Dad ever said anything to you?" Marcus asked.

"No."

"Well, Do you want to know for sure?"

That question cracked something open for me. I didn't even think about that.

"I don't even know who I am. " I whispered. "I've always felt like he treated my sisters a little differently, a little better. Now I'm wondering if that's why."

Marcus turned fully toward me.

"You are not your mother's mistakes," he said. "No matter who you are or what your last name may be, know that you are a gift from God."

That was it. That was the line. The one that made my eyes overflow. Because I had been carrying my mother's choices my whole life.

And suddenly.... I didn't have to.

Marcus said exactly what I needed to hear. As tears rolled down my face, his words made me feel closer to him than I ever had before. He wiped my tears with his thumb, looking at me like he wished he could take the pain away. Seeing me cry and hearing how lost I felt broke his heart.

I could see it in his eyes. He hated that he couldn't fix my problems. All he knew to do was hold me in his big, muscular arms. In his arms, I felt safe. I felt genuine empathy. The tears fell uncontrollably at that point. He lifted my chin so I could look at him while he spoke. My heart felt like it had intertwined with his.

He was saying something like:

"Everything will be okay..."

But I barely heard the rest. Before I knew it, I stood on my tiptoes and leaned in for a kiss. It was long.

Passionate.

Overdue.

I didn't just need him.

I wanted him.

I was ready to go to the next level. Marcus gently grabbed my face and pulled back.

"No," he said softly.

"I don't want our first time to happen under these circumstances."

For a second, I just looked at him and then I smiled. He probably thought I was reacting from the pain or just because he was there for me at that moment. I appreciated him even more at this moment. He wasn't trying to take advantage of me but I already knew he wasn't that type of man. This wasn't about pain and sadness, for me this was about clarity and that's one thing I have right now!

It was time. I'm ready!

I leaned in again, slower this time. Intentional. My hands slid up his chest until they rested around his neck. "I'm not confused, " I whispered. I'm not doing this out of pain or confusion. I'm doing this because I want you. His eyes searched mine, making sure.

"I want you," I said softly.

Something shifted in him then.

The restraint.

The hesitation.

It melted.

When he kissed me again, it wasn't rushed. It was deep. Slow at first — like he was still giving me time to change my mind. His hands rested at my waist, firm but controlled. I didn't pull away. Instead, I stepped closer.

The kiss grew heavier. Warmer. Months of tension finally releasing. His hands moved to my back, pulling me into him, and I felt the strength in his arms wrap around me like protection and desire all at once.

It wasn't wild.

It wasn't careless.

It was chosen.

When he lifted me slightly and walked us backward toward the bed, my heart pounded — not from fear, but from certainty. For the first time in my life, I wasn't reacting to chaos. I was moving toward something real.

When we finally crossed that line.... It felt like the beginning of something.

Not a mistake. Not confusion. The beginning.

When everything finally slowed, the room felt different. Quieter. Just silence. Not awkward silence. Full silence. The kind that only happens when two people feel safe. My fingers traced lazy circles across his chest, feeling the steady beat of his heart under my palm.

"I meant what I said," he murmured after a while.

"I know," I whispered. He didn't roll away. Didn't reach for his phone. Didn't rush the moment. Marcus stayed right there. His arm draped over my waist, our legs tangled, our breathing slowly finding the same rhythm. For a while, we didn't say anything.

Another pause. Then the talking started — soft at first. They talked about how long this had been building. About how he almost said something months ago.

"You know you almost ruined it by pretending like you weren't feeling me." Marcus teased. "You know you couldn't resist these pretty brown eyes."

I nudged him. We both busted up laughing.

The next morning, I woke up before him. The room was still dim, soft morning light peeking through the curtains like it didn't want to interrupt us. For a second, I didn't move. Marcus' arm was draped across my waist, heavy and warm. His breathing was slow, steady against my shoulder. One of his hands rested near my collarbone like it had settled there in the middle of the night and decided to stay.

I smiled to myself.

No rush.

No tension.

No questions.

Just us.

I carefully turned my head to look at him. His face looked different when he slept — relaxed, unguarded. No jokes. No smooth lines. Just Marcus. I want him to be mine!

The thought made something flutter inside my chest. I shifted slightly, and his arm tightened instinctively, pulling me closer without him even waking up.

"Mmm," he murmured, eyes still closed. "You're not going anywhere."

I laughed softly, "I wasn't trying to."

His eyes opened slowly, adjusting to the light. He looked at me for a long second — not speaking — just taking me in.

"You good?" he asked again.

That question was simple and gentle. It wasn't a concern, it was tenderness.

"I'm better than okay," I said.

"And I meant it."

He leaned forward and kissed my forehead — slow, unhurried — like we had nowhere else to be. We laid there talking about nothing important. Breakfast. Music. Whether Shanice was already taking selfies at the airport. Whether Mr. Landcruiser snored on the planes.

It was light.

Easy.

Normal.

A few minutes later, the intensity softened into something lighter. He pulled the blanket up and said, "So... does this mean I finally get promoted from 'friend'?"

I smacked his chest lightly with a grin. "Don't get ahead of yourself."

He smiled.

And just like that, the heaviness broke. The laughter wasn't loud. It was soft. Content. As I laid there with my head on his shoulder, I realized something:

For the first time since my mother's phone call...

My mind wasn't racing.

It was still. And that's what made it special. For once, my life didn't feel complicated.

It felt simple.

When I finally got up to shower, I glanced back at him stretched across the bed, with his socks still on, watching me like he still couldn't believe I was here.

"What are you thinking about? I asked. You're just smiling."

He grinned wider.

I walked into the bathroom smiling too!

CHAPTER 7

GOD BROUGHT IT BACK

The choir had just sung their final selection. I was feeling good spiritually, lifted by the music. The harmonies still echoed in the sanctuary when Pastor Johnson stepped up to the pulpit. His sermon felt personal — like he was talking directly to me. One line, in particular, settled deep in my spirit.

"God is finished giving you milk. It's time for meat. Protein."

For some reason, those words took me back.

Milk.

All the milk God had fed me throughout my young life — situations I survived that should have broken me. I felt like at that moment God was saying I had graduated. That He had been with me through it all. That I knew I wouldn't have made it without Him. Now it was time for something heavier.

Stronger.

Because I was stronger.

And my mind drifted back to one of the hardest days of my childhood.

My dad had just dropped us off after spending the weekend with him. The minute his car pulled off, my mom began her usual interrogation. What did we do? Who was over there? How did his girlfriend treat us?

We answered honestly. His girlfriend had been mean, spiteful, unpleasant as usual — but nothing we said deserved what came next. My mom called my dad and told him to come back.

At first she sounded concerned, like she cared about how we were treated. But slowly her tone shifted. She began adding details we never said happened. When my dad looked at us for clarity, I denied the lies.

That's when everything escalated. The argument intensified fast. Voices rising. Accusations flying.

Then my mom grabbed an ashtray and swung it at my dad. It hit. His mouth instantly filled with blood — so much blood I couldn't even see his teeth. It was running down his chin onto his shirt. I don't know who he was angrier at — us for telling the truth, or her for hitting him. I saw rage in his eyes as he stepped toward her, but then he looked at us and walked away. He slammed the door behind him.

And then...

She turned on me.

She grabbed me by my hair and threw me onto the couch. Her fists landed over and over — my face, my neck. I kicked. I screamed. I tried to push her off, but she was stronger. She began choking me, her anger spilling out in every hit. My younger sister stood there crying, frozen, too scared to move. Eventually my mom's boyfriend pulled her off of me and dragged her into their bedroom.

For a few seconds, I couldn't breathe. My body ached. My chest burned. My throat felt tight.

"I can't take this anymore," I whispered to my sister. I grabbed a plastic grocery bag and stuffed it with my panties and bras. That's all I thought to take. I told my sister to do the same. The front door was literally steps from my mom's bedroom.

"On the count of three, Sis... we're running and we are not looking back."

"One, Two,Three!"

We flung the door open. I ran. Jumping two or three steps at a time down the stairs. My heart was pounding in my ears. Then I heard my mom yelling behind me, telling my sister to stop me.

That's when I realized.... She wasn't with me anymore.

It was just me. Me against the world.

I turned the corner and saw the gas station across the street. I ran inside and straight behind the counter, grabbing the cashier's leg, holding on as tight as I could.

"Call the police! Please call the police!" I cried.

"She's going to kill me! I'd rather go to jail than go back home!" I screamed.

My mom bursted in the store seconds later, yelling my name like I was crazy.

The police arrived. She lied calmly. Said I went ballistic over punishment. Said I was acting out. My sister stood there silent — too scared to speak. I wasn't mad at her, I understood her fear. At that point, I was the stupid one for trying to be brave and leave. I begged the officer.

"Please. Just take me to jail. Anywhere but home." He put me in the back of his car. For a moment, I felt relief. But instead of driving away, he drove me back across the street. Back to her. She dragged me inside and grabbed an extension cord. She whipped me again — my arms, my legs, my back, my thighs. The cord left bruises, blue and red, some had cut the skin. There were so many marks that I lost count.

———

Days later, we visited my dad again. This time I was angry.

"How can you say you love us but let her keep hurting us?" I asked through tears.

"Look at what she did to me!"

I lifted my shirt. Turned around. Showed him my back,my legs and arms.

His eyes filled instantly.

"I didn't know it was that bad," he said, pulling me into him. "I'm so sorry."

That was the day he decided to fight. CPS was called. They took pictures of every bruise. Every cut, every welt. Temporary custody was granted. But the fight wasn't over.

———

The trial was the scariest day of my life. The judge called my sisters and me to the stand.

His voice was soft. Gentle. It helped — but I was still terrified. Before my name was called, I whispered a prayer.

"Lord, help me. I really need you right now. Please open the doors to a safe, loving home for me and my sisters. Amen."

The judge asked us how each parent disciplined us. "Who did we want to live with and why?"

My hands shook. My voice cracked. But once I started talking, something shifted.

I told everything. The beatings, the bruises, the days she didn't allow me to eat because she was mad. The nights I cried myself to sleep. For the first time, my truth had a microphone.

During the lunch break, my sisters and I went to the restroom. The door slammed. It was my mom. She stormed in, pushing us against the wall, cursing, accusing us of lying. Fear flooded my body again. What we didn't know was that a court employee was in a stall and heard everything. It was immediately reported. When court resumed, everything changed.

My dad was awarded sole, full custody. Even as the gavel hit, signaling my father's victory, a quiet thought settled inside me: survival was no longer just about escaping. It was about knowing my worth, speaking my truth, and protecting myself — in every part of life. If I could stand there, trembling yet unbroken, I could face the storms ahead. I could fight for love, for respect, and for the life I wanted to live, on my terms.

———

At that moment, I cried, tears of joy, tears of relief, tears of peace because I didn't have to think about committing suicide if I had to go back with her. I didn't feel like running anymore. I didn't feel like hiding. I felt free. Sitting there in that courtroom, I realized something. Running away didn't save me. But telling the truth did.

I survived. I fought. I sought justice.

The milk was gone. It was time for meat, Protein! Strength.

And somehow… I had it.

Pastor Johnson is still preaching about the symbolical term for meat. Monique zoned back off and realized something:

Jail didn't save her. The police didn't save her. Running didn't save her. But she's still here. She's sitting in a pew. Dressed. Whole. Breathing.

That little girl who ran across the street thinking jail was freedom?

She grew up and she did not become the woman she ran from. That strength, born of fear and pain, would follow me. It would shape how I loved. How I forgave. How I chose. One day... it would guide me when my heart demanded more than my past allowed.

I snapped back, realizing I had survived more than I ever gave myself credit for.

As I wiped the tears from my face, there were sounds of hands clapping, voices rising, people shouting, "Amen."

CHAPTER 8

WALKING INTO SOMETHING

It was my favorite time of the week — packing a bag and heading to L.A. The weather was perfect. Not too cold, not too hot. Lisa and I were headed to Venice Beach. There was a celebrity basketball tournament going on, and Shanice was meeting us there. Lisa had plans after the tournament, which was cool because I was spending the rest of the weekend with Shanice. Her mom wanted me to go to church with them Sunday. I loved going to Shanice's house. They always had good home-cooked meals, and her grandparents and mom were so nurturing. It felt peaceful there.

“Girl, hurry up! ” Lisa yelled. “I’m not trying to miss the game sitting in traffic. “I might find my future husband on the beach!”

I laughed. “I’m almost done!”

We were rolling down the 405 blasting music, singing and rapping to whatever came on the radio. By the time we got to Venice, it was packed. Food stands lined the boardwalk, the smell of fried food and kettle corn floating through the air. Kids were running around, and people formed circles around street performers hoping to earn a few dollars. Waves crashed behind us while music blasted from somebody’s radio. It felt like everybody and their mama was outside.

I was really feeling my outfit today, and I guess others were too! I wore my yellow daisy dukes with black biker shorts underneath, a black halter top to match. A mixture of yellow and black slouch socks that popped with my black Adidas. I wore my hair curly that day. I didn’t feel like worrying about it getting messed up near the water.

There were plenty of cute boys trying to holla at me. They asked for my telephone number, but everyone was getting the wrong number. I had enough to figure out with the two men on my plate now. Lisa and Shanice teased me, saying I was acting like an old married woman turning down some of the finest guys out there.

We watched a few games, rode bikes, and shopped a little. Lisa and Shanice even got tattoos. I was too scared. The look on their faces while the needle hit their skin was enough for me to politely decline. By the time it got dark, the beach started clearing out. Lisa left for her hot date, and Shanice and I headed to the Shaw. The Shaw was like the after-party to the beach. Same crowd — just relocated. People cruising down Crenshaw, music blasting, hanging out in parking lots.

Shanice was being Shanice — double parking, running red lights just to trail someone she thought was cute, making U-turns wherever she felt like it. The whole night felt electric. It would have been perfect if I had run into Marcus. Passing by the Wienerschnitzel made me think of him.

We got back to Shanice's house a little after 1 in the morning. You would think we would go straight to sleep considering that we have to get up at six to get ready for church but we didn't. Shanice and I stayed up talking about the Hawaii trip, Mr. Landcruiser and of course Marcus.

It seems like we just dozed off when we were awakened to Shanice's mom knocking on the door telling us to wake up and get ready for church. "I smelled bacon drifting through the house. "We ate and left the house by 7:15am. I don't know what it is but going to church seems like it gets my week off to a good start. The choir was jamming! I was standing up clapping and singing along to every song. While the preacher was giving his sermon, my purse started vibrating, Marcus had paged me the numbers 1 177155 400 following. (Back then that was the way to say I miss you.). After seeing that page, my mind was distracted from the sermon. Couldn't tell you what the preacher was talking about. My mind was on Marcus. I had to see him again before I headed back home. I'm going to call him as soon as I get to Shanice's house.

After church was over lunch was already prepared at Shanice's house. Her grandmother had cooked a meatloaf, cabbage, macaroni and cheese and cornbread early that morning before church. All we had to do was change our clothes and wash up to eat. Oh my God, the food was delicious! After we finished eating, Shanice and I were ready to go pay Mr. Landcruiser and Marcus a visit. Normally Marcus and I met at the hotel, but this time he invited me somewhere different.

For the first time, I was going to see where he actually lived — his grandmother's house. I was nervous and excited to see him all at the same time. Marcus opened the door, and the look in his eyes immediately made me blush. For a moment we just stood there smiling at each other before he stepped aside.

"Come on in," he said.

I glanced back toward the car where Shanice and Mr. Landcruiser were already pulling away to grab something to eat. Shanice had told me she'd be back in a little while, leaving me to go inside alone.

The house felt warm and quiet as I stepped in behind Marcus. In the living room, his grandmother sat watching television. A small fold-up table was set up in front of her with a bowl of diced watermelon resting on top.

"Grandma," Marcus said, walking over to her, "This is Monique... my girlfriend."

The word "girlfriend" caught me off guard, but I smiled politely.

"It's nice to meet you," I said.

His grandmother looked me over, for a moment before breaking into a smile.

"She's a pretty little thang," she said, turning her head toward Marcus.

Then she looked back at me.

"Marcus must really like you. He's never brought any girl to the house before."

I felt my cheeks warm again and glanced over at Marcus, who looked entirely too pleased with himself.

After a moment, his grandmother returned her attention to the television, reaching over to pick up another piece of watermelon.

Marcus leaned closer to me and whispered, "See... I told you she'd like you."

I nudged him lightly. "You didn't tell me you were going to introduce me like that."

"Like what?"

"As your girlfriend."

He shrugged like it was the most normal thing in the world.

"You are my girlfriend." "You will always be mine." He said confidently.

Hearing Marcus introduce me as his girlfriend caught me off guard. The strange part was... it felt good. For a brief moment, I even caught myself wishing it were true. I looked over at him, still surprised that he said that in front of his grandmother. Marcus loved and respected her deeply. If there was one person he wouldn't lie to, it was her. Which meant he probably meant every word he said.

Marcus walked toward the kitchen and motioned for me to follow him. When I stepped inside, he opened the refrigerator and grabbed two sodas.

"You want one?" he asked.

" Yes, thank you."

Our fingers brushed when he handed it to me, and neither of us moved right away. For a moment we just stood there looking at each other.

"You're blushing again," he said with a quiet laugh.

"I am not."

"Yes you are." He said smiling.

I shook my head and tried to change the subject, but the smile on my face probably gave me away.

Even with his grandmother sitting in the living room, the space between us felt different. The way he looked at me made everything feel softer, quieter. Marcus leaned back against the counter and folded his arms.

"So when are you going to stop acting like you don't like me?" he teased.

I laughed. "Who said I don't like you?"

He stepped a little closer.

"I can't tell," he said. "You got that look."

"What look?"

"That one right there."

I rolled my eyes and turned away, but he gently reached for my hand before I could walk out of the kitch-en.

His voice lowered. "Monique... I'm serious."

The way he said my name gave me a chill through my body. I slowly turned back around to face him.

"For real?" I asked, trying to keep my voice steady.

He nodded, his eyes not leaving mine.

"For real." He said

For a second, I didn't know what to say. Everything in me wanted to laugh it off... brush it away like it wasn't a big deal.

But it wasn't.

"I don't know..." I said quietly, glancing down at our hands.

"Don't know what?" he asked.

I shrugged a little. "If I'm supposed to be doing this."

"Doing what?" He said calmly.

"This..." I said, looking back up at him. "Us."

He studied my face for a moment, like he was trying to understand everything I wasn't saying out loud.

"Ain't nothing wrong with this," he said softly.

I let out a small breath. "It's not that simple."

His thumb moved lightly against my hand.

"It can be," he said. "You're just making it complicated."

I shook my head. "No... life makes it complicated."

For a moment, neither of us said anything.

After a while, his grandmother pushed herself up from the couch and grabbed her purse.

"I'm about to run to the store before it gets too crowded," she said, glancing at Marcus. "Y'all behave while I'm gone."

Marcus chuckled. "Yes ma'am."

Once the door closed behind her, the house grew quiet. Marcus looked over at me and smiled before reaching for my hand and gently pulling me up from the couch.

"You didn't give me my hug today," he said.

I laughed softly and stepped closer to him. When he wrapped his arms around me, the hug lingered a little longer than either of us expected. When we finally pulled back, our eyes met. For a moment neither of us said anything. Then he leaned in slightly. I didn't move away.

The space between us disappeared, and before I knew it, we were kissing. When we pulled apart, hearts beating fast, we both laughed a little, almost like we were surprised at ourselves. Marcus rested his forehead lightly against mine. When we stopped Marcus was staring into my eyes.

"You are something else. I don't know what it is about you, but..." Marcus paused, shaking his head sideways.

"What do you mean?" I asked.

“You gotta figure this out!” he said.

I lowered my head.

“I know...” Just give me a little more time.

Because as good as this felt... I want more. He said.

“I know you’re engaged to ole boy, but...” He gave that mannish smile. “...I think you really want me. You’re just playing hard to get.”

I tried to roll my eyes, but the smile on my face gave me away.

“You’re just that confident huh?,” I teased.

For a moment we just stood there, still close, his hands resting lightly on my waist while my arms were around his neck. Then he kissed me again.

This time, neither of us held back. The house was quiet, and the longer we stood there, the easier it was to forget everything else—the church service, Shanice being gone, even the fact that his grandmother could come back at any moment. All I could think about was him. The way he looked at me. How good he smelled. The way he held me.

Before long, one kiss turned into another, and the space between us disappeared. We got lost in a moment neither of us had planned but neither of us wanted to stop. We both knew it couldn’t last long—but that only made it more enticing. Anyone could come back through that door at any moment but at that moment, we didn't care.

———

We finally pulled away from each other, our breaths heavy, hearts still racing, yet smiling from the physical sensation. I stole one last look at him, memorizing the curve of his smile, his muscular body, the way his eyes lit up when he looked at me.

"I gotta go," I whispered, barely able to get the words out while trying to catch my breath.

Shanice, my ride waiting outside, and the world beyond Marcus brought me back to reality.

He nodded, though his hands lingered on my waist for just a moment longer.

"Page me when you get home," he said softly, almost like a command disguised as a plea.

"I will," I promised, smiling even though my stomach was full of butterflies.

Walking out the door, I felt a strange mix of excitement and jitters. Part of me wanted to stay in that moment forever, lost in Marcus' arms but I couldn't. I had to face reality and go home. Shanice was waiting in the car, munching on some fries, oblivious to the mixture of feelings swirling inside me.

On the way home I had to tell her what happened—how I met his grandmother and how he introduced me as his girlfriend.

"Girl, I was nervous for nothing. His grandmother was nice. I can't believe she left us alone in her house."

"I know you were being fast, thinking you're grown once she left," Shanice teased. "Y'all need a whooping!"

We both busted up laughing.

"Girl, it was worth the whipping," I said, and we gave each other a high five.

"How were things with Mr. Landcruiser?" I asked.

"Well... we didn't have as much fun as you did," she smirked.

The ride home went by fast.

"Yes it did," Shanice said. "I gotta come inside and use your bathroom before heading back."

"Okay cool. I'm going to grab the shoes and purse you wanted to borrow."

When we walked up the steps, I noticed from the window that the lights were on in my living room.

Hmm... maybe I left them on by mistake, I thought.

When I turned the knob, I realized the door wasn't locked. Both of us knew something wasn't right. Shanice and I looked at each other instantly. We knew what time it was. We started taking off our earrings, pulling our hair back.

We pushed the door open slowly, bracing ourselves just in case we had to fight.

CHAPTER 9

IT WAS GETTING REAL

Once the door opened all the way, we noticed the TV and the lights were on throughout the house. Before we could even process that... Our eyes went straight to the sofa.

"Hey baby... I'm home." It was Lamond.

He was stretched out on my sofa like he had been there all day, watching TV... eating my Chocolate Chip Cookie Dough ice cream straight from the carton.

"Hey baby, I'm home." he said casually, glancing over his shoulder.

I froze. I wasn't ready for him to be here yet. I needed more time. My chest tightened so fast it felt like the air had been knocked out of me. For two years I had imagined this moment. I thought I would scream, cry, run into his arms. None of that happened.

Instead the first thought that crossed my mind was Marcus. The perfect day we just had. His pretty brown eyes. His touch. The way he looked at me like I was the only woman in the room.

Just like that, the excitement I thought I would feel for Lamond... wasn't there. Shanice let out a little laugh, trying to match the excitement Lamond expected to see on my face but when she looked at me, her smile faded. She could feel the shift in the room.

"Mo..." she said quietly. "You good?"

I swallowed hard and forced a smile but inside, my mind was still somewhere else. Still in Marcus' arms.

Deep down, I realized something I wasn't ready to admit out loud. Lamond had finally come home but my heart was no longer waiting for him.

"Hey, Shanice, I'll walk you out to your car. I needed some air anyway — plus this was my chance to call Marcus, like I promised."

"Thanks for having my back, Shanice. I didn't know who was in my house."

"Girl, you know I got you," Shanice said.

"I appreciate that. What should I do about Lamond... and Marcus?"

"Follow your heart and the signs that lead you to happiness," Shanice replied with a wink.

"Shanice, can I use your phone real quick to call Marcus? I left mine on the bed while grabbing my purse and shoes for you to borrow.

"He told me to call when I got home."

I could feel the knot in my stomach tighten as I dialed. Too bad the call would come with bad news.

"Hey, Marcus."

"Hey," he replied warmly.

"I made it home safely."

"Oh yeah? That's good. I hate you had to leave so soon... I miss you already."

Shanice shot me a look, silently saying, Be careful.

"Yeah, I hate it too! I had fun with you. But... I have something to tell you."

"What's up?"

"When I came home... Lamond was in my house." I paused, holding my breath. A long sigh came through the phone.

"Man... I knew this was going to happen. As soon as I started really falling for you, Ole Boy showed up. So I guess it's no more us, huh?"

My head dropped. "Yeah," I whispered, though it squeezed my chest to say it. I could hear the hurt in his voice — it mirrored my own.

"My grandmother is calling me. I gotta go." Click.

Shanice, usually joking, looked genuinely sorry for him.

———

It had been the longest, most miserable week of my life. Lamond had taken over my space, laid out across the sofa, eyes stuck on the TV, phone to his ear, tearing up everything edible in sight. Nothing was put back. Nothing was cleaned. Every corner reminded me he was there.

The hardest part wasn't even the chaos. It was the weight in my chest knowing I had to end things with Marcus. Every time I thought of him, my stomach tightened and a headache pressed at my temples.

Lamond noticed the shift in my mood. He tried to pull me close more than once, but I pushed him away. Not because I didn't care about him at one point, but because I couldn't betray Marcus in my heart. Lamond assumed it was just moodiness — maybe even that time of the month so he gave up for the moment but I could feel his frustration simmering under the surface.

One day while Lamond was in the shower I grabbed Lamond's dirty clothes from his tote bag to make a complete load to wash. I noticed some letters tucked in his tote bag. A woman, talking about a baby, there were pictures too! My stomach dropped. I felt sick. Part of me wanted to scream. Finally, I couldn't take it anymore. I grabbed my phone and dialed Marcus. My hands shook, my chest thumped like a drum. I needed to hear his voice.

"Hello?"

"Hey..." My throat tightened.

"Mo? Are you okay?"

"I... I just needed to hear your voice."

A pause. Then his tone tightened. "Where are you at?"

"Yeah... it's been stressful. I can't... I just can't take him being here. I don't want anything with him," I admitted.

Marcus's voice softened, tinged with hurt. "Mo... I wish you could just be free from all that."

"I know..." I whispered, almost crying. "I'm trying... but it's hard."

"Promise me something," he said quietly. "Promise you won't let him get to you. Do what's right for you, not for me, your mom or even him. Think about what makes you happy,

“I promise,” I whispered.

We stayed on the line a little longer, just talking, just sharing our voices. Hearing him grounded me. Made Lamond’s presence feel even heavier.

When I finally hung up, a mix of relief and ache settled over me. Relief because I heard his voice. I ached because I was still trapped in my house seeing Lamond’s face, living a life I no longer wanted. I feel stuck if I end things everyone would say, I’m a failure they would laugh at me. I can almost hear my mom‘s voice, telling me how stupid I am for letting him go and that no one would ever love me any better. One thing was crystal clear: my decision was made. I wanted to end the engagement. I no longer wanted to be with Lamond. I wasn’t that same girl who allowed him to cheat on me. Now I had to come up with a plan to get him out of my house.

Lamond stretched out on the sofa, phone pressed to his ear, flipping through channels with one hand, eating a bag of chips with the other. He didn’t even notice me at first.

"Hey, baby..." he said finally, looking my way with that same sly grin he always wore. "Why so quiet? You look... different."

I swallowed hard, forcing a smile. "Just tired, that's all."

He scooted closer, stretching an arm across the back of the sofa. "Come sit with me. Let's hang out. We haven't had time together."

I stepped back instinctively. "I... I don't feel like it."

He raised an eyebrow, confusion turning into annoyance.

"Why not? You used to love being around me."

"Things changed, I've changed. I'm not that same girl, you left when you went to prison." I bit my lip, my mind flashing to Marcus. I thought about how we like the same type of movies and laughed at parts that others wouldn't think were funny. How time went by so fast when we were together as though there was never enough time. He took the time to get to know and like the real me. Lamond doesn't know the real me anymore.

"It's... complicated," I said, keeping my voice calm, though my chest burned.

Lamond didn't give up. He leaned in closer. "Complicated? Come on, Mo. We're engaged! We should be spending intimate time together. We should be making up for lost time." "Why are you treating me like I did something wrong, like you're mad at me?"

I shook my head. "I'm not mad. I just... I can't do this."

His grin faltered. "Can't do what?"

"Pretend." The words just slipped right out my mouth.

"Pretend that I'm okay with any of this. Pretend like I don't have feelings... feelings for someone else."

For a second, he froze, like he didn't understand. Then he laughed, nervously. "Someone else? Girl, you trippin." Who?"

I stared at him, heart hammering. "That's irrelevant."

The air between us thickened. Lamond's pager beeped, and he ignored it, clearly trying to gauge my reaction.

He leaned back, rubbing his face, frustration creeping in. "You're acting... weird. What's wrong with you?"

"There's nothing wrong with me. You just can't seem to handle the truth."

"You haven't told the truth! I am your first, your last and your only." It took almost everything in me not to yell at him; "to go back to wherever he came from. Just leave." I was trying my hardest not to be mean, but I gotta come up with a plan to end this engagement, this relationship, quick!

CHAPTER 10

ENOUGH IS ENOUGH

It was Friday, time to go to LA. I had my bag packed and ready so that I could head straight out there from work. Shanice and I were invited to a pool party, and I planned to stay in LA for the weekend. I didn't bother telling Lamond that I would be gone. However, I did notify Marcus that I would be out there as usual.

The party was fun. It felt good to get away from Lamond for a while. I didn't get to see Marcus this weekend because he was scheduled to work, but that was okay. I got to talk to him each night, and hearing his voice soothed me. As we headed back to my house, I thanked Shanice.

"Thanks for letting me spend the weekend with you. Girl, I needed this getaway. Lamond has been getting on my last nerve."

Shanice looked over at me.

"I don't know why you chose him over Marcus."

"Technically, I didn't have a choice," I said.

"Yeah… you're right," Shanice replied.

When we pulled up, I exhaled with relief. "Whew, I'm glad we made it. I have to use the bathroom."

"Me too!" Shanice said, jumping up and down trying to hold it.

I laughed. "Girl, you go first. You look like you have to go more than me."

When it was finally my turn, I went into the bathroom. While I was there, I could hear Lamond talking in the living room. At first it sounded like a normal conversation. Then his tone changed.

"Damn Shanice," he said. "I see you got thick! When are you gonna let me take you out on a date?"

My blood instantly started boiling.

For the first time, I realized something clearly—Lamond hadn't changed at all.

"Boy, you better stop playing with me," Shanice snapped. "That's disrespectful."

"Disrespectful is you acting like you don't want me, Shanice,"

Lamond shot back. "You've always wanted to get with me. You saw how good I treated Mo and you were jealous."

"Yeah right," Shanice said with a laugh full of attitude. "I've never seen anything good about you! I don't even see what Mo saw in your trifling behind."

Then I heard it. A loud smack. Followed by yelling.

I rushed out of the bathroom just in time to see Lamond standing in Shanice's face after slapping her. Something inside me snapped. Before I could even think, I jumped on his back.

"Get off her!" I yelled.

Lamond reached back and slung me over his head, throwing me to the ground. He tried to slap me, but I blocked it. Then suddenly his hands were around my neck. The pressure tightened so fast it almost knocked the air out of me. Shanice jumped into protector mode. She grabbed a broom and started hitting him with the stick end.

"You better let her go!" she yelled, swinging again and again.

The blows made him loosen his grip. Somehow Shanice jumped on his back and wrapped her arms around his neck in a headlock. They stumbled and crashed to the floor. Everything was happening so fast. Then we heard my neighbor yelling from outside.

"Monique! Are you okay?"

"No!" Shanice yelled back. "I need help!"

"I'm calling the police!" the neighbor shouted.

That was enough. Lamond managed to break free, jumped up, and ran out the door.

A few minutes later the police arrived. They took our statements and asked if we wanted to press charges.

"Yes," I said without hesitation.

While one officer was writing everything down, another officer came over. They said they had someone nearby who matched Lamond's description and asked if I could identify him. I got into the police car and rode up the block with them. They had Lamond pinned against a gate handcuffed near some apartments. I stayed in the back seat of the patrol car. When he turned his head, our eyes met. For a moment, everything inside me froze. Part of me wanted him to pay for what he did. Another part of me just wanted this whole chapter of my life to be over. The officer looked back at me.

"Is that him?"

My throat tightened.

"No," I said quietly. "That's not him."

As the police car drove away, my eyes stayed on Lamond until I couldn't see him anymore.

The house felt too quiet. Shanice left, so now it's just me and my thoughts. Today was something else. Too many things occurred in one day. After everything that just happened, I should've felt relieved that Lamond was gone. I finally had my space back. But for some reason... I felt drained, lost, confused, and maybe even a little lonely. As I layed on the sofa flipping through the channels on the TV, nothing seemed appealing enough to take my mind off my problems. Too bad I don't drink or smoke—it might've helped alter my mood. After going through all the channels again, I gave up. I decided to take a bath.

I walked into the bathroom, turned on the water, and let the tub fill up. I didn't even bother turning on the bright light. I just lit a few candles and placed them on the counter next to the sink. Just enough to relax my mind and body. I needed something to calm me down. No more chaos. I grabbed my radio and put in my self-made mixed cassette tape of my favorite R&B songs. It had a lot of songs that matched how I felt.

Once the tub filled, I sunk down into the water and leaned my head back against the edge. For a moment, I just sat there. Quiet, still, then I let out a long breath.

"God..." I whispered.

I paused, shaking my head a little. "I don't even know what to say." So many thoughts with so little words. My eyes stared up at the ceiling, but my mind was everywhere.

"I don't know how I got here."

My voice cracked a little.

"I thought I had everything figured out. I thought I was doing the right thing... trying to be a good woman, trying to build something real." I swallowed hard. "But this, Lord... this is not what I pictured." I closed my eyes, feeling the bubbles move slightly around me.

"Lamond... Marcus..." I whispered their names like I was trying to make sense of them.

"I don't even know what I'm doing anymore."

A tear slid down the side of my face, mixing with the water.

"I've been through too much when it comes to men. My daddy... Lamond..." I let out a small, tired laugh and now this."

I shook my head slowly. What do I do now? Apparently what I thought was right for me wasn't.

"I don't even trust my choices anymore."

My chest tightened.

"I don't know who I'm supposed to be with… who I am… or if I'm even supposed to be with anybody right now."

I just sat in my thoughts for a second. Then my mind drifted to Marcus. Just saying his name made my stomach bubble up a little bit.

"I didn't expect him. I didn't plan for that but the way he makes me feel… is different."

I paused.

"But nothing about this situation feels right."

"Lord… is he the person you have planned for me?"

The room felt still. Like everything was waiting. I took a deep breath.

"I just need your help… your guidance."

My voice dropped to almost a whisper.

"I need you to show me what to do about Marcus… about my life… about everything."

Another pause.

"Lord, please… just give me a sign." " In your name I pray. Amen"

I sat there in silence, letting the water move around me, the music playing softly in the background.

Waiting.

CHAPTER 11

THE TRUTH WAS IN THE BAG

Marcus had the day off, so he stayed in bed a little longer than usual. Not because he was sick or anything like that. His mind was just a million miles away. He lay there with his arms folded behind his head, staring up at the ceiling. He was a little burnt out from his visitor that came last night. Marcus let out a slow breath.

"Now that Monique is single..." he whispered to himself. "I want her to be my woman. I want to make it official... but I gotta tell her."

He shook his head slightly.

"God, if you're listening... help a Brutha out!"

His eyes shifted across the room for a brief moment, like something had pulled his attention, but he quickly looked away.

"I hope this goes well," he muttered. "Mo ain't about to see this coming..."

He paused, thinking about her. The way she smiled. The way she looked at him.

"Yeah... I gotta tell her,". he said finally.

Then he reached for his phone and made the call.

———

At work the next day, I was bagging a customer's groceries when the phone rang.

"Front desk, Monique speaking. How may I direct your call?"

" You don't have to direct the call anywhere, but you can direct yourself to me."

An instant smile came across my face.

"Hey," I said, trying not to sound too excited.

"Hey... I know you're at work, so I'm not gonna keep you long," he said. "I know you're coming out here tomorrow, but can you come straight to my house instead of going to the hotel or Shanice's?"

"Why?" I asked.

"I gotta talk to you about something," he said.

He paused.

"Something important."

The rest of my shift went by slowly. Too slow! My mind kept replaying his words. Something important. What could he possibly have to tell me that he couldn't say over the phone. Marcus has never asked me to come to his house instead of our normal spot at the hotel.

"Hmmm, this must be pretty serious. Maybe he thinks Lamond might come back. Maybe it's too much for him so he wants to end things face to face."

I did ask God for a sign. "Could this be it?"

By the time I clocked out, my nerves were already all over the place.

———

The bus ride to LA felt longer than usual. I tried to calm myself down, but my thoughts wouldn't stop racing. Part of me got excited and another part of me felt nervous. I'm trying to think positive. The only thing that's helping me feel better is my prayer from the other night.

Is God giving me clarity of what to do with my love life?

———

When I finally got off the bus, I stopped at the liquor store to grab a soda and some candy. I'm going to need something to snack on because I'll be too shy to eat in front of his family. When I walked up to Marcus's house, everything looked normal. Too normal, which made me really nervous. Trying to shake this feeling in my chest. Then I finally got the courage to ring the doorbell after smoothing down my hair and double checking that my clothes were nice and straight . As I walked up to the door, I noticed how quiet it was. I didn't hear his granny's voice, the TV, music or anything.

A few seconds passed. Then I heard movement inside. My heart started beating fast.

The door unlocked.

And then...

It opened.

———

Marcus stood there with a weird, uneasy look on his face. Before I can ask him what's wrong?

My eyes dropped instantly.

To the baby in his arms. Everything inside me froze. I couldn't even blink. My eyes were glued to the baby. I was lost for words. Was my eyes playing tricks on me? The baby was small, drinking his bottle, looking around like nothing in the world was wrong.

Peaceful.

Unbothered

And for some reason.... I couldn't stop staring.

"Hey...". Marcus said softly.

I stepped inside slowly, still trying to process what I was looking at.

Hi, Hello to you too! Marcus said sarcastically.

“Hey…” I finally said back, my voice barely there.

I tried not to stare too hard. I tried to act normal but I couldn’t. It was something about that baby that had me puzzled. I can’t pinpoint what it is but he seems familiar.

Marcus closed the door behind me.

“I know this is probably not what you expected,” he said but let me explain.

I let out a small sigh.

“No… it’s not.”

So again, whose baby?

Marcus looked down at him, then back at me.

“He’s mine.”

My heart dropped.

Not from heartbreak but from the shift. Everything was changing. Right in front of me.

“Oh…” I said quietly.

I felt like the wind was punched out of me.

“I didn’t know how to tell you,” Marcus continued. I just found out not too long ago myself.”

I nodded slowly. Still trying to catch up.

“What’s his name?” I asked.

Marcus smiled a little.

Markel... Marcus said with a smile.

Something hit me, hard! That feeling again. Stronger this time. My stomach dropped and a headache came instantly. I don't know why I'm feeling this way.

This is a feeling I can't shake off. It's an unexplainable feeling. This baby looks so familiar. I know I saw him somewhere before. I just couldn't place it.

"Who's his mother?" I asked, my voice got a little tighter now.

Marcus hesitated for a quick second.

Then he said her name..... Tiffany Hays.

And just like that...

Everything clicked.

The letters.

The pictures.

The baby, the mother's name.

My head started throbbing at this point.

That baby... I remember where I saw him now. In Lamond's bag. I swallowed hard, trying to keep my face calm. Trying not to let everything I was thinking show.

But inside.... Everything was clicking. I stared at the little boy in Marcus's arms, my mind racing as all the pieces finally started coming together.

And in that moment...

It all made sense. God revealed something I didn't expect.

As I sat there, still trying to process everything I had just discovered, I couldn't help but watch Marcus with the baby. He was so patient. So attentive. So gentle. If I ever had a baby one day... I could see him being a good father, but I always imagined being the one to give him his first... and his last child. That thought alone did something to me. Seeing Marcus with that baby became too much! I couldn't take it. I don't want a relationship with someone who already has kids. I don't have time for baby mama drama.

I didn't stay long. I used catching the bus as an excuse to leave. I gave Marcus a kiss... and walked out the door. I barely made it down the street before the tears started falling. I couldn't hold them in anymore.

"I can't believe this..." I whispered to myself.

Just when I thought things were finally about to go right for me.... Here comes more pain. More confusion. More drama.

The more I try to love against the pattern of bad relationships... the more I seem to fall right back into it.

My chest tightened.

Could that baby really be Marcus's?

Or...

Am I right?

Could Lamond be the father?

My mind started racing.

CHAPTER 12

TWO LINES

Out of all the people in the world, could it be true that Marcus and Lamond were with the same woman? How could Lamont do this to me? After everything I went through with him...

After trying so hard to stay loyal... He was out here cheating the whole time? Possibly making babies!

Then another thought hit me. Why would he propose to me? Nothing was making sense.

The whole ride home, I was there physically...but mentally, I was somewhere else.

All I could see was Marcus...Holding that baby. Then the letters came back to me. The pictures, the names,

Tiffany Hays and baby Markel. My heart started beating faster.

I couldn't wait to get home to go through everything in Lamond's bag. I'm going through every letter, pictures and anything he left behind and never came back for. I swallowed hard and opened the first one.

By the time I made it home, my chest still felt tight. I grabbed Lamond's tote bag and dragged it to the living room floor. I sat in front of the bag and started digging for any information I could find.

"Why am I doing this?" I whispered.

But I already knew. I unzipped it slowly. The smell hit me first.

His favorite cologne.

I pushed past it and started digging through clothes, random papers. Nothing that mattered.

Until... I saw them... the letters.

My stomach dropped instantly. I pulled them out, my hands started to shake. The same handwriting. The same name at the bottom. Tiffany Hays. I swallowed hard and opened the first one. "I miss you Baby..."

My eyes moved faster now.

Scanning, searching

"...I wish things were different...".

"...he deserves to know..."

I froze.

"He?" I whispered.

My heart started racing. I grabbed another letter.

Flipped it open.

"...Markel has started to say Dada. I hope he will get to look you in the face so that you can hear it one day."

That name again. My chest tightened.

"Markel", I said, while shaking my head.

I dropped the letter slightly and reached deeper into the bag.

That's when I saw them.

The pictures.

My hands hesitated for a second before picking them up. But once I did...

I couldn't stop staring. It was the same baby. The same little boy I just left.

My heart started pounding so loud I could hear it.

"No..." I whispered with my hands covering my mouth in disbelief.

Picture after picture. Different days, different outfits but same baby.

My stomach turned.

I flipped one picture over and there was writing on the back.

It read; "Markel, three months.

I closed my eyes tight for a second. Trying to compose myself, but it was too much!

Marcus holding that baby. The letters, the names, the pictures all collided at once.

"This doesn't make no sense..." I whispered.

But deep down.... It was starting to. Too much of it was lining up. Too much of it felt connected. I sat there on the floor, surrounded by pieces of a story I didn't even know I was part of. For the first time... I wasn't just hurt. I was starting to feel something else, embarrassed dumb, used! " I should have known better."

I lost track of time going through all those letters and viewing pictures. I don't know how I ended up knocked out on the sofa asleep. I was tired, mentally and physically.

I woke up to the same horrible headache from last night. I hopped in the shower, hoping that would help wake me up. I decided to run across the street to the fast food restaurant to grab something to eat so I could take something for the headache.

I was standing in line, looking at the menu, trying to figure out what to order. "Hmmm... a Denver omelette sounds good." I placed my order with the lady behind the counter. She said, my number—28, will be called when my meal is ready.

As I waited for my number to be called, my stomach started growling. It sounded as if I hadn't eaten in days. I rubbed my stomach while looking around, hoping no one heard it.

"Number 28!" the lady yelled.

I walked to the counter to get my food, but then suddenly I felt nauseous. The room went black. That's all I remember. When I woke up, I was in the ambulance headed to the hospital. I could hear someone saying my blood pressure was low, but I couldn't open my eyes. After fully gaining consciousness, the nurse was standing over me with a cotton swab under my nose.

"Where am I?" I asked, completely confused.

"You're in the hospital," the nurse answered. "The doctor will be in to talk to you in a few minutes."

I nodded my head. There was a knock on the door.

"Hello, Ma'am. I am Dr. West. How are you feeling?"

"I'm feeling a little better… I'm just confused about why I'm here."

"Well, you fainted at the fast food restaurant, and the paramedics brought you here." The doctor said, looking over his glasses at her.

"Oh, okay," I replied, nodding.

"So I have some good news and bad news. Which would you like to hear first?"

"The bad news first," I said.

"Okay, the bad news is your iron is a little low, so I'm going to prescribe you some folic acid pills to take care of that. The good news is your blood work also shows you're pregnant. You're going to be a mother. Congratulations!"

"Pregnant? Me? Are you sure?" I asked, shocked.

"Yes, Ma'am. Your HCG levels indicate you're pregnant."

"Are you serious?" I asked again, still in disbelief. "No disrespect to you, doctor, but can we do another test?"

"Absolutely," he said. "I'll send a nurse in here to collect some urine. We'll conduct the test right in front of you."

A few minutes later, the nurse came back with a pregnancy test that she placed right next to my urine sample on the counter.

"Have you ever taken a pregnancy test before?" she asked.

I shook my head and said, "No."

"No problem. It's really simple," she said. "One line means negative—you're not pregnant. Two lines mean you are pregnant."

"Okay... got it," I said, my hands trembling.

What felt like a long time was only a few seconds. My heart was beating fast.

I can't believe this... me, a mother. I looked back down at the two lines.

Ring, ring.

My phone rang. It was Marcus. I looked at his name on the screen, and the two lines in my hand. I sat there for a long moment, taking it all in.

I looked at his name on the screen...

and the two lines in my hand. I didn't even know what I was supposed to do... tell Marcus the truth or go find Lamond and get answers first.

The more I try to love against the pattern of bad relationships... the more I seem to fall right back into it.

But maybe, just maybe...

God was giving me a chance to do it differently this time.

Epilogue

The house felt... familiar, but not in a good way. More like the kind of familiar that brings back stuff you never really dealt with.

I sat across from my mom, my hands resting in my lap. She hadn't said much since I walked in.

She was just watching me. Like she was trying to read me without asking too many questions.

"You okay?" she finally asked.

I let out a small breath.

"Yeah... I think so."

But honestly? I didn't even believe that myself.

She tilted her head a little.

"You look like you got something on your mind." She said,

I nodded, "I do."

The room went quiet again. One of those silences that says more than words.

Then she spoke.

"Have you talked to him yet?"

My head started to itch. I already knew who she meant.

"No," I said.

She nodded like that was the answer she expected. Another pause.

I looked at her. Really looked at her.

"How long did you know?" I asked.

She frowned a little.

"Knew what?"

I swallowed.

"About my dad."

That did it! I saw it in her face. The shift. The hesitation. She looked away.

"It's complicated," she said.

I let out a small laugh. Not even a real one.

"Yeah..." I said. "I'm starting to see that."

Without even thinking, my hand moved to my stomach.

She noticed, of course she did.

Her eyes dropped to my hand... then slowly came back up to my face.

Just like that, everything changed.

"Are you pregnant?" she asked.

I hesitated for a second.

Then I nodded yes.

She didn't react the way I thought she would.

No look of excitement.

No questions.

Just a look.... One I couldn't quite explain before but now? I understood it.

She leaned back in her chair, quiet, thinking.

Then she said:

"Life has a way of repeating itself..."

My chest tightened.

Because for the first time.... That didn't just sound like something she was saying. It felt like a warning. I sat there, my hand still resting on my stomach.

Thinking about Marcus, Lamond and everything I didn't have answers to.

At that moment,

I had to ask myself something I wasn't ready for.

Was I really about to break the pattern or continue to follow it?

Author's Note

This story is more than just a story for me.

It's a reflection of real emotions, real situations, and real choices that many of us have faced at one point or another. Loving the wrong person, ignoring the signs, holding on to what feels familiar—even when we know it's not right.

Writing this book forced me to look at things differently. It made me think about the patterns we fall into, the things we accept, and the moments when God is trying to redirect us—even when we don't fully understand it at the time.

Sometimes, it's not just about the person we love—it's about the words we've heard, the things that were said to us, and how deeply they affected how we see ourselves. Emotional wounds, especially from people we love, can make us feel like we're not enough... like we can't do any better... and before we know it, we find ourselves settling for less than we deserve.

Monique's journey is about more than love. It's about growth. It's about learning how to let go, how to choose better, and how to trust God even when everything feels confusing.

If you see yourself anywhere in this story, just know you're not alone.

Breaking patterns isn't easy. Choosing differently isn't easy. But it is possible.

Give yourself grace. Trust the process. Most importantly, don't ignore what God is trying to show you.

This is only the beginning.

— LaKisha Ridley

Author's Bio

About the Author...

LaKisha Ridley is a storyteller who writes about love, relationships, and breaking unhealthy patterns. Her work focuses on emotional growth, self-reflection, and the journey of learning to make better choices.

She is a wife, a mother and a woman committed to growth, faith, and living with purpose.

Loving Against the Pattern is her debut novel—

and the beginning of a story that is far from over.

Follow her journey as the story continues in Book 2 of Loving Against the Pattern.

www.ingramcontent.com/pod-product-compliance
Lightning Source LLC
La Vergne TN
LVHW010903110826
845149LV00005B/1460

9798995924708